Mel snagged his lapels, tugging him toward the dance floor.

She fit her palms to Xander's back pockets and sank into a hip-grinding shimmy that placed her taunting features at his zipper level. Enough was enough. He jerked her up so they were eye to combative eye, then sent her spinning and reeled her back with a snap that knocked her against his chest. While she grasped for breath, he gave her a look so filled with the promise of sinful excitement, it lit her enthusiasm like a backfire in the brush.

And then she released a breathy laugh that dropped right to his loins. "What's a conservative like you know about dancing like this?"

"I wasn't always a conservative. I was...more."

Mel felt his grin as he gave her a taste of what he'd been. Fun, she decided. He'd been fun. A daredevil. Like her.

Exhilarating.

Dangerous.

Dear Reader,

Location, location, location! Setting a book in the right place sometimes makes all the difference. I had the characters, the plot but not the place until a conference in Reno and a side trip to Lake Tahoe. Nothing like having someone in a pickup truck tailgating you down a mountainside at forty miles per hour with no guardrails to get the creative juices flowing!

Warrior for One Night was a thrill ride to write. I loved every page, creating one of my favorite heroes out of nearly fifty books. Even had to take him along on my cruise, where I was busy working on chapter 8 on my suite balcony at 5:00 a.m., waiting for the sun to rise, and while proofreading on the floor of the Miami airport. I'll have to put those pictures up on my Web site!

Hope you enjoy this latest!

Happy reading!

Nancy Gideon

Nancy Gideon

WARRIOR
FOR ONE NIGHT

Silhouette

Romantic
SUSPENSE

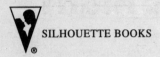

SILHOUETTE BOOKS

ISBN-13: 978-0-373-27532-8
ISBN-10:   0-373-27532-3

WARRIOR FOR ONE NIGHT

Copyright © 2007 by Nancy Gideon

Visit Silhouette Books at www.eHarlequin.com

Printed in U.S.A.

NANCY GIDEON

Portage, Michigan author Nancy Gideon's writing career is as versatile as the romance market itself. Her books range in genre from historicals and regencies to contemporaries and the paranormal. She's a *Romantic Times BOOKreviews* Career Achievement in Historical Adventure and HOLT Medallion winner and a Top Ten Waldenbooks series bestseller. When not working on her latest plot twist at 4:00 a.m., when her writing day starts, or setting depositions at her full-time job as a legal assistant, she's cheerleading her sons' interests in filmmaking and R/C flying, traveling (for research purposes, of course!) and rediscovering the joys of single life. Visit her at www.TLT.com.

For my Road Warrior writer trio, who helped me tackle the ups, downs and almost off the edges of Lake Tahoe. Laurie, the Indie wheel who kept us from a *Thelma and Louise* ending, Loralee, who thankfully said she was afraid of going up in the gondola first, and Lana whose wet wipes saved my shredded bacon. Thanks, ladies!

Prologue

She couldn't breathe.

Smoke seeped in through the car's vents, changing the air into something that tasted hot and raw and clawed all the way down.

From where she was belted in the Nova's tiny back seat, she watched the ridge with mounting apprehension. It was lit with a bright sunset glow. And they were heading toward it, not away. Her mother never looked at it. Her fierce concentration was on the road ahead.

What was wrong? What could be worse than the approaching flames?

All morning Melody had watched her mother and the fire with equal dread as both built and grew more combustible. They could smell the acrid heat pulsing against the cheap walls of their motel as June Parrish paced and panted like a wild thing trapped at the edge of the blaze. She'd held a bag of ice to the ugly welt on her cheek as her frantic gaze cut between the silent phone and the door where all their belongings sat stuffed into the three duffel bags. For the hundredth time, she checked her wristwatch. Each passing minute added to her agitation. Finally, her mother stopped her restless movements and gave a savage sigh.

"Damn him."

The curse exploded from her like boiling sap from the forest pines. She threw the ice to the floor and grabbed the bags.

"Come on, baby. If he's not coming to us, we're going to him. Get Karen."

Heat from the parking lot hit, a solid wall. Melody ran to the room next door where she and her fifteen-year-old cousin had spent the night. They'd huddled together in the big bed in the dark, trying not to hear the sounds of an esca- lating argument in the other room. Three years older and a lifetime wiser, Karen hadn't let her check to see if her mother was all right, even after the angry storm settled into a silence that was somehow…worse. They'd gotten no sleep, afraid of the fire sweeping down on them, terrified of the violence on the other side of the thin wall.

Karen had her single bag in hand. Her features were somber and somehow ancient, but she managed a tight smile as she banded the younger girl's shoulders with a squeeze of support. The car was running. Karen climbed in front and Melody in back, next to their battered cooler and her father's extra gear. They tore out of the driveway in a spit of gravel. Heading toward the flames.

The resort was a huge, hillside-hugging building hewn

from native logs. Fuel for the fire. Ground pounders were on the roof, wetting it to protect against the deadly embers floating down on the hot wind. In their protective gear, one firefighter looked pretty much like the next. June pulled into the paved parking lot where the night before a half-dozen pumper engines had sat waiting to go into the field along with a single helicopter. The copter was still there. Hope surged within Melody as she gripped the back of the seat in front of her.

"Is Paddy coming with us?" Even at a young twelve, she called her father by his name—at his insistence.

Her mother answered with a brusque "Stay in the car."

The two girls did as they were told, sitting anxiously while the stench of smoke and grit slowly gained a stranglehold on them within the hot interior. They coughed, their eyes fixed on the long front porch and beginning to tear up. Then Karen reached for her lap belt.

"Mama said to wait."

Karen's tone was as harsh as the stuff they were trying to inhale. "You wait. I'll be right back." She slipped out of the car and raced up to the building, now backlit in an eerie glow.

The minutes passed. Melody hugged the bucket seat. She'd been raised to pay respect to the flames as if they were some unpredictable animal that was warm and friendly one moment then lunging with teeth bared the next. And she'd been taught to listen. But her mother hadn't listened when she was told to head down the mountain in a hurry. She hadn't taken the girls home where they'd be far removed from the danger massing on the other side of the ridge. So why should she?

As she got out of the back seat, brushing ash from her

hair and eyes, Melody took a choking breath and simply stared in dismay. The left wing of the empty resort was no longer dark and abandoned. Light gleamed behind the wall of windows. A bright, flickering, fearsome light.

It was on fire.

"Mama! Karen!"

She ran up the many steps to the front porch and inside without a thought to her own safety. Her family was in there.

Smoke roiled down the hall, thick, black, deadly. Flames rimmed the door frame like a circus hoop. And she stood frozen, praying her mother or cousin would come jumping through it.

"Mama? Karen?"

A faint cry answered, female and afraid.

Covering her mouth and nose with the sleeve of her T-shirt, Melody ran toward the sound, crouching low. The heat was tremendous, prickling over her exposed skin as she ducked down the hallway. Her tears seemed to sizzle on her cheeks.

"Mama? Karen? Where are you?" she shouted, forcing the words through the searing thickness in her throat.

"Melody! Help me!"

Karen.

The room was swirling with smoke. Flames licked along the exposed ceiling timbers, eating through them with an insatiable hunger. She could hear them cracking over head as she stumbled through the choking haze.

And then she saw her cousin on the far side of the room. She lay sprawled on the floor beneath one of those huge beams. Her fingers were clawing at the floorboards as she tried to pull herself out from under it. Her face was a mask of terror and pain. Her eyes were on Melody.

"Help me, Mel! For God's sake, help me!"

She started forward just as an ominous groaning sounded above her. She glanced up to see a huge decorative chandelier made of canvas and elk horns plummet toward her, a fireball. Screaming, she lunged back. The fixture hit like a comet, crashing into the floor, scattering debris and flame everywhere. The carpet ignited, becoming a sheet of fire. And on the other side, her cousin began to shriek.

There was no way across the room. No way to reach her fallen cousin. As her head grew light, starved by lack of oxygen, Melody remembered the men on the roof. If she could get their attention, have them turn their hoses...

"Melody! Don't leave me! Mel!"

She burst out onto the porch, gasping, desperately afraid she'd succumb to the smoke before she could save her cousin. She stumbled down the steps, staggering into the front yard, where neatly groomed flower beds were beginning to wither and fry. She waved her arms and tried to call out for help, but her lungs seized up into a harsh paroxysm of coughing. She could hear screaming over the roar of the blaze, knowing it was the sound of her cousin, her best friend, roasting alive.

"Down here! Help me! There are people inside! Help me!"

One of the smoke wreathed figures on the roof began to turn.

Melody's legs buckled. She went down on hands and knees, dizzy, gasping, sobbing. Through the grit filming her vision, she could see the forest on fire. As she swayed, fighting to stay conscious, she noticed something moving toward her from the back of the heavily timbered hillside, up between the evenly spaced tree trunks. It whirled to the edge of the trees and there it stopped, a ball of fire that took on a humanlike form with arms and head above the swirl of flames. It made a sound that raised the singed hair on the back of her neck, a sound like a woman screaming. The fire devil danced wildly before her horrified gaze, a frenzied dervish, then fell apart among the flames.

And that was the last thing Melody Parrish remembered.

Chapter 1

"What the hell was that? Mel, what's going on up there?"

"Nothing. Be down in ten. Everything's under control."

Five minutes ago she wouldn't have been lying.

Jimmy Doolittle once supposedly said there was no good reason to be flying near thunderstorms in peacetime. But then Jimmy had never fought against a lightning storm in a helicopter by dropping water from a Bambi Bucket.

She'd been in the air for five straight hours, swooping down through a double rainbow only once to take on fifty gallons of Jet A fuel. Thunderheads continued to gather mass in the surrounding quadrants, making it harder to dodge around the clouds. Rain battered against her windshield as the ride grew bumpy. When the call came to pull back, she ignored it, shifting her headphones

from her ears to ring about her neck. And she kept
working, beating back the flames one hundred gallons at
a time. Wind swirled around the Long Ranger, hitting her
from every possible direction as she went down for
another dip. She'd taken the front door off for the water
drop and leaves were blowing around in the cockpit.
After putting in some big power changes to maintain
altitude, she had started to worry. But she didn't second-
guess her decision to stay. There was no way she'd let the
fire beat her.

She'd stayed in the air as darkness gathered. Knowing she
had to be on the ground by 8:55 p.m. or face the wrath of
the Bureau of Land Management safety gods, again, she dismissed the terse order to call it a night. She had until thirty
minutes past sunset to make every second count. Then it was
Miller time, not before. With position and instrument lights
on, she followed her GPS heading. She was on the radio to
her crew chief when halfway up the canyon, a thousand feet
above the ground, at seventy-five-percent torque and ninety
knots, she smacked into a solid wall of air.

The impact threw her into her shoulder straps. She heard
a loud thump followed by the whine of rotor RPM decay-
ing. Thinking it was engine failure, she lowered the collec-
tive while a million things ran through her mind. Should
she turn the routine call into one of distress? Start emergency procedures? Was she going down? But then the
rotor RPM came back and with a gust of relief, she realized
she was still in control. Elated to get through what left too
many aircraft looking like confetti, she sped on to Lake
View, where the ground had never felt better.

With the blades still making a lazy circle overhead, she

hopped out of the cockpit to toss her helmet to the older man waiting there.

"That was close," she told her uncle as they both ducked low to trot out of the rotor wind. "I must have hit a micro burst or wind sheer. Bam. Like a brick wall. Make sure you give her a good once-over before we go up again to see that nothing was rattled loose."

"I can tell you what's rattled loose," came another angry voice. "Your brain, that's what. What the hell were you doing up there, Mel?"

Taking a breath to maintain her calm, Mel turned to face Quinn Naylor, her boss and long-ago, one-night lover, with a disarming smile. "I call it flying, Quinn."

"By the seat of your tight pants," he shouted back at her, not in the least appeased by her levity. "I call it reckless. I thought I made myself clear when I brought you in on this gig. There's no room in the air for any John or Jane Wayne heroics. That's not how I run my show."

"I was getting the job done," she yelled back at him, giving up on civility to go toe-to-toe on the tarmac. She was an impressive five-ten in her La Sportiva boots, but he had a good five inches of tightly compacted fury on her.

"Not with my crew. Not anymore. Go home, Mel. I'm pulling your ticket."

Too angry to feel shock or distress, she pushed into his face with an aggressive snarl. "Take your crew and shove it. I'll catch another ride."

"No, you won't."

The flat, brutal way he said that finally cut through her arrogant pose. She knew a moment of reassessing regret, but it was seconds too late to stop the rest of his decree.

"No one's going to call you up, not even when the only thing they have left to throw at the fire is spit. You're a menace up there, Mel. You're dangerous and you're unreliable, just like your old man."

Then, in a soft voice that was somehow so much worse than his screaming of minutes ago, he repeated, "Go home, Mel. There's nothing for you here."

She turned away from him, furious, frightened and too prideful to let him, of all people, see it. "Thanks for nothing, Quinn." She didn't need charity from the likes of Quinn Naylor. And she didn't need to invest heart and soul where she wasn't appreciated. She gripped her uncle's arm and tugged hard. "Come on, Charley. Let's go."

As she stalked away, her reluctant crew chief uncle in tow, Quinn yelled after them, "Tell Karen hello for me."

"I'll do that, Quinn," Charley agreed affably and was almost pulled off his feet for his troubles.

As she stuffed her few belongings into her duffel, the magnitude of what had just happened settled in deep and dire. She paused, leaning on her palms on the edge of the bed, panic swelling inside until her head ached with it. Until her eyes swam with it. What if he was true to his word? What if he got her blackballed from doing contract work in this, the height of fire season? When she was counting so desperately on the money to keep their business afloat? To keep them afloat.

What had she done?

"Don't worry, Mellie." Her uncle's big hand fell warm and comforting on her shoulder. "You and Quinn just always seem to rub each other the wrong way, but I can't believe he'd turn his back on our friendship."

"I hope you're right, Charley." For all their sakes.

But he wasn't. The next morning proved Quinn Naylor a man of his word. There was no work to be found, no crew that would have her, even with pilots scarce and long hours looming. She had every door politely but firmly closed in her face until all that was left was a disgraced retreat. She wouldn't go begging. No matter how bad things got. If that was what Naylor was hoping for, he could wait until this particular hell froze over.

"We'll get by," Charley vowed with his eternal optimism. But he wasn't the one paying the bills. He wasn't the one writing the checks, hoping the bank would clear them. He wasn't the one looking over the long list of debts owed, dividing them into piles of can-wait, not-yet, and last-call. They needed to make repairs. They needed to pay their insurance premium. And it would be nice to have something in the refrigerator other than beer and tortillas.

"We'll find a way," she assured him with a confidence she was far from feeling.

She wasn't one for belief in miracles. Especially when she opened the door of her makeshift home in the back of their hangar and started picking up the scattering of mail strewn about the floor. Bills. Second Notice. Final Notice. She sorted and tossed them one by one into the wastebasket by the door. Problem solved. For the moment. Then, she caught sight of the light blinking on her answering machine. Hoping it was a crew leader having come to his senses, she hit playback.

"Ms. Parrish, my name is Jack Chaney. I'm looking for a pilot with a lot of moxie. If you're looking for a job that pays a helluva lot more than you're making now, give me a call."

"What's that all about?" Charley asked, observing her odd concentration.

"I'm not quite sure. Maybe just the life ring we need to keep us from going under for the third time."

She'd made the follow-up call to Personal Protection Professionals out of curiosity. What would a private protection agency want with someone like her? But after talking, first over the phone, then face-to-face, with its owner and badass operator Jack Chaney she got to thinking that maybe, just maybe, she was in the right place at exactly the right time. Chaney was looking for someone to do piloting security work on an on-call basis. The money was good. The money was actually great—and just the infusion of life-sustaining capital to support her and her uncle's air charter service until Quinn Naylor saw fit to give her a break. There was nothing in the short assignments to get in the way of the everyday operation of Wings of Fire. And Chaney clinched the deal by paying off the balance on her overdue insurance to keep her airborne. She had the talent and the tools and he had the connections. A marriage made in bartering heaven.

Four weeks later, feeling silly in her formfitting flight suit with its howling wolf logo stitched over her left breast, with her licensed weapon tucked almost as an embarrassment under the seat of her Bell Long Ranger, she set down in Las Vegas to pick up her first assignment. Newly trained in firearms skills, hand-to-hand, surveillance and the legal ins and outs of employing any of those methods under the guise of a bodyguard she felt strong and confident in her new role. Until she got her first look at her client.

Xander Caufield, an insurance specialist carrying a fortune in rare stamps to an exhibit/trade show in Reno. That didn't sound too dangerous. Or exciting. She was to ferry him wherever he wanted to go and keep him and the contents of his locked case safe. Not exactly shuttling military secrets. Old stamps were about as thrilling as the envelopes she'd tossed into the waste can. She couldn't imagine any high-level intrigue going on there. But it was her first sizable paycheck, slotted to cover her fuel bill, and she would take it as seriously as the number of zeroes ahead of the decimal point.

She waited in the broil of the midday Nevada sun as a sleek limo approached, fighting the impulse to shade her eyes to get a better look at the man stepping out of that big backseat toting a metal courier case and a garment bag. With the glare off the hardtop, all she could discern were polished shoes and an immaculate suit. The first thing that impressed her, because she couldn't see his features, was the way he moved. He had a quick, aggressive step implying no hesitation in wherever he was going. An all-business stride. Together with the expensive suit, that got her hot-guy Geiger counter ticking away at a brisk pace. Then he crossed into the shade of the Ranger and the needle went off the charts.

He was *Maxim* gorgeous. Dark, styled, but in no way soft. Chiseled masculine features, a heavy slash of brows, uncompromising mouth and a direct stare that could probably bend steel bars. She caught herself before wetting her lips but allowed an inner *rowl-rowl*. His gaze touched on her briefly as she came forward to greet him, her hand extended to take his bag.

"Mr. Caufield, I'm Mel Par—"

"Let's go. I'm in a hurry."

She rocked back on her heels as he strode by, her brows lifting slightly. Aware that her hand still hung in midair, she scrubbed it against the other one and let both fall to her sides. "All righty then. Welcome aboard, buckle up and we'll get airborne."

He climbed up into the copter, giving her a glimpse of a monumentally nice butt. But since he was acting like one, her interest cooled considerably. Sometimes good looks just couldn't overcome bad manners. A shame.

He settled into the back, draping his suit bag over one seat, strapping into the other. Situating the case between his elegantly clad feet, he looked purposefully out the window. Dismissing her as if she were invisible.

Great. See if she'd offer the in-flight movie.

After a quick preflight check and a chat with the tower, she had them up and off the flat Vegas desert.

The flight was silent and uneventful. Easy money. Because small talk with her coldly gorgeous passenger was off the table, she fiddled with the radio, trying to pick up chatter on the latest blaze chewing its way through remote California forest land, heading for her back door. So far, they were trying to contain it with backfires and burnouts, but it was proving to be a tricky beast. Dry conditions and high winds had it skipping and shifting one step ahead of their best efforts to suppress it.

Listening to the dispatcher and the back-and-forth banter, a fierce longing to be in the thick of it had her clenching her teeth and calling down all manner of ills upon Quinn Naylor. It didn't matter that she had a job, that her time was well paid for by her arrogant passenger in back. If she thought there was the slightest chance she could zip over the state line and be toting hand crews and hotshots from dawn until dusk, she'd have pushed Mr. Xander I'm-too-damned-important-to-give-you-a-polite-nod Caufield out the back door to let his glacial attitude warm a bit out in the sun and sand. But that wasn't going to happen and Caufield's comfy ride was guaranteed for the moment.

And it didn't hurt that he was so easy on the eyes.

She settled back in her seat and tried to calm her mood toward her meal ticket.

Mel appreciated affluent men…from afar. She enjoyed fantasizing about those almost too pretty glam boys in the designer suits who attended the theater and drove cars with unpronounceable names. The ones who wore silky scarves or pastel sweaters draped around their necks for no apparent reason and had their nails done. After a long day in the air, after sharing raucous laughs and longnecks with the crew, she found herself imagining what it would be like spending the evening with a man who didn't smell of smoke and sweat, who didn't pepper his sentences with profanity and fire acronyms, who could talk about something other than weather systems, fuel management and the closest available waitress with big hooters. A man who didn't live from season to season on a puny GS rate that hardly covered the bets laid down at the pool table. One who could take her to a restaurant that didn't serve hot wings as the main entrée.

The men she knew were her drinking buddies, her co-workers, and not the stuff of romantic dreams. In the air and on the ground, they were heroes. Up close, they tended to be petulant, obnoxious, controlling or just plain more trouble than they were worth. She didn't actually know what she'd do with one of those swanky cover boys if he stepped off his pedestal and into her rather grimy check-to-check existence. But she did like ogling them. And Caufield was worth a long, long look.

She glanced back at him in her mirror. He was staring straight at her, and from the furrowed concentration of his brows, apparently had been for some time. That intense and not quite flattering study gave her a sudden chill. She wasn't unfamiliar with men's attention. She'd had them stare at her in lust, in anger, in warm camaraderie. But this was none of those things. His look was as sharp and precise as a surgeon's blade and her pulse jumped in alarm. What on earth had she done to deserve a slashing tribute from a man she'd never met, didn't know and had no intention of getting to know better? Maybe he didn't like to fly. Maybe he didn't like women who flew. Maybe he didn't like women. Whatever his problem was, it was giving her the creeps.

Reaching up, she snagged the curtain that separated the cockpit from the back and jerked it closed. Still, she felt the prickle of his stare and was glad to crest the mountains to see the soup bowl of Reno below with its handful of resort hotels sticking up from the desert floor like dominoes. Great. Her first assignment and she was stuck shuttling some weirdo with an attitude and issues. And a great butt.

A car was waiting. She had to jog to get ahead of her client to efficiently open the door. He didn't look at her, merely tossed his bag in first before sliding into the cool, dark interior. He paid her no attention until she climbed in to take the opposite seat. His surprise was evident in the widening of his eyes. Hazel eyes, with mysterious hints of green. They were gorgeous, too.

"Door-to-door service," she explained. "Part of the job."

"You don't really need—"

"Yes, I do."

She pulled the door shut, ending any further protest. When push came to shove, she could be rude and undiplomatic, too.

He smelled good.

It was a short hop to the hotel, which bordered the airport. In those brief minutes, the chilly limo filled with the faint scent of whatever exotic cologne he was wearing. It had her nose twitching and her meter ticking again. Because there was nowhere else to look, she found herself studying his hands. Clean, long fingered with neat nails. Not pale as she would have expected from a high-rise type, but lightly bronzed. Probably the tanner rather than the true outdoors. No wedding ring or sign that he'd ever worn one.

She felt his stare and slowly let her gaze lift to meet it. His directness unnerved her, and she was sure he knew it, but she matched it unflinchingly for a long silent minute. Then, feeling rather silly with their stare down, she broke the stalemate.

"Will you be needing me again tonight?"

"No. I'll see you have an itinerary in the morning."

She nodded. How frigidly professional of him. He had a nice voice, clipped but low, soft and a little gruff around the edges. In other circumstances, sexy as hell. Who was she kidding? Everything about him was sexy as hell. Except his attitude.

They pulled into the hotel circle, and again he gave her

a questioning look when she climbed out with him. She relieved him of the need to ask.

"As long as you have that case, consider us Siamese twins."

He didn't smile. He didn't betray any displeasure. She began to wonder if he had a pulse.

She stood slightly behind him at the check-in desk, aware, without being distracted by the surrounding chaos of the casino behind them, of everyone within snatch-and-grab range. She didn't offer to hold his bags. She wasn't there to be his porter. She was there to protect his butt. A delicious duty had there been a little shorter stick up it.

When he had his key card in hand, she walked close to his elbow as they wound through the game floor. The noise and lights and mill of gamblers made her edgy. Nervously, she went over all that Chaney and his instructors had taught her about being ready and vigilant and…damn. She'd left her pistol under the seat of the Ranger. A lot of good it would do there if some collector-stamp junkie leaped on them from behind the nickel slots. Feeling sheepish, she adjusted her walk into ultra tough chick mode, hoping that would be enough to discourage anyone from a tussle. It must have worked, because no one approached them. Or it could have been the arctic blast exuded by Caufield.

The elavator doors closed and up they went. Just as she started to relax, she could see him give her a quick once over in the reflective strip above the door. Nothing flatter-ing about it.

"Tomorrow, do you think you could wear something a little less…obvious?"

She didn't turn. Instead, she met his gaze in the polished bronze. Her teeth bared in what he couldn't mistake as a smile. "Whatever you like, Mr. Caufield. Would you prefer business casual or escort service?"

The corners of his mouth twitched, and suddenly, she wanted to see his smile. She bet it would do glorious things to the sharp bone structure of his face. But no such luck.

"I'll leave that up to your discretion."

She marched him down to his room and slipped in first to give it a brief but thorough check, acting as if she'd performed this task with countless clients more important than himself. At her nod of all clear, he entered, hanging his garment bag in the closet and tossing the case on the bed. It gave a slight bounce on the taut spread and Mel wondered in wildly unprofessional and inappropriate curiosity how it would feel to take a similar bounce on that bed beneath Xander Caufield. Like being pressed between an iron and ironing board, she assumed, dismissing the fleeting fantasy with a grim smile.

"If you need me—"

"I have your cell number."

He was levering out of his shiny shoes, peeling his socks off with them. As his bare toes curled into the nap of the carpet, a purely salacious chill raced through her. He was staring at her again, this time with slight impatience.

"Good night, Ms. Parrish."

There was no reason to linger.

He latched the door behind her and released his pent-up breath. Slipping out of his jacket, Xander let it drop carelessly over the back of the desk chair before he settled on the edge of the bed. He snapped the catches on the case and pulled out the contents he'd brought with him. A fat insurance file and the real reason he was in Reno.

It wasn't about stamps.

Chapter 2

Sipping the bottled water that came with his delivered meal, Xander leaned back on the bank of pillows he'd wedged against the backboard of his bed. He was wearing only his suit pants, needing the chill of the climate-controlled air against his bare chest and feet to keep his weary senses sharp. He opened his file and spread the reports across the bedspread to give them closer study. He had them memorized, but there was always the chance that he'd missed something. The way he had that afternoon.

His pilot wasn't what he'd expected and he didn't like to be surprised. Mel Parrish should have been a man. When she'd told him her name, he'd been knocked off balance, with all his preconceptions askew. The quick glimpse he'd dared take of her while scrambling for his composure revealed the worst. Young, attractive, female. How had those facts gotten under his radar? Need-to-know facts to a man who prided himself on details.

Her being a woman opened up a whole different avenue upon which to discover what he needed to know. But it didn't change the facts in the file.

He was tracking an arsonist for hire. One who lit a torch for the insurance money. One who either used or created fires to cover his fraudulent activity. In the past seven years, Western Mutual Insurance had paid out in the billions for properties that went up in smoke. The policy owners all had something in common—a serious financial glitch that was solved by the influx of cash. Cash handed over by Western Mutual because they couldn't prove any wrongdoing. And that made them decidedly displeased.

That's where Xander came in.

He was the best there was at what he did. Meticulous, relentless, ruthless. He'd made his reputation on those three things. And upon his track record of always uncovering the truth. That's how he could demand the price he did. A sometimes hard-to-swallow percentage of the policy payout. Money they would otherwise kiss goodbye. Money that didn't really matter to him. It was the process and the end result that he enjoyed. He liked the challenge and he had to win. That's why the companies came to him with the cases they couldn't solve themselves.

For five years, he'd immersed himself in the minds and means of those who thought to cheat the system. He'd start with the obvious. Who had the most to gain? Then he'd follow the money. He didn't work in an office, not after the first phase of investigation. He excelled in the field. Blending into the lives of those who thought to get away with a payout they didn't deserve. He'd get close, he'd become their friend, their partner, their confidant and sooner or later, every time, they'd slip up and he'd have them. Infinite patience was its own reward.

Only in this case, the reward wasn't his hefty fee.

Restless with his lack of progress, he set aside his hand-written notes and made a call on his cell. He made it a practice of never using traceable land lines. There wasn't much he trusted, except the person who answered his call of "I'm in." And the response was the one he'd been waiting to hear.

"Got another e-mail. We're talking money. It's showtime."

Xander smiled thinly, trying not to react to the sudden lunge of anticipation. The chase was on. "Don't be stingy, but don't be too eager. We don't want to scare him off."

"Hey, don't tell me how to deal with criminals, pal. It's what I do."

Kyle D'Angelo was a security expert. They'd gone to prep school then college together. He was the one friend Xander could claim with no strings attached, with no what's-in-it-for-me agenda. He was the one person who'd suffered him as a fool, who'd seen him at his lowest and hadn't turned away. Money couldn't sway him. Hard times hadn't discouraged him. During the wild years, he wasn't the one Xander called to bail him out of a tight spot. Because Kyle would be there seated at his side saying, "Damn, that was fun." He was the closest thing Xander had left to family. And it was Kyle who'd brought him the precious lead he'd been searching for for five frustrating years.

His call came out of the blue. Always happy to hear from him, Xander hadn't expected the reason to be busi-

ness. Cut-right-to-the-soul-of-him business. Kyle was in-
stalling security in Lake Tahoe at a posh resort/casino
whose owners had gotten a little too lean in the pocket to
complete the astronomical renovations they'd started.
They'd been contacted a month ago. A terse e-mail from
an undisclosed sender. The message was brief.

I can make your money troubles go away.

At the first hint at rising from the ashes with the insurance money, Kyle had placed the call that he knew would
mean everything to his best friend. Then he had used his
resources to help Xander get next to his prime suspect.

"You just let me know when you're ready to set the trap."

"Not just yet. I need some time to make sure we're
stalking the right game." A discomforting truth. For the
first time, when the stakes were their highest, he was going
on the hunt woefully unprepared. He had only the rudi-
mentary research done, and while that told him he was
using the right bait, he didn't know what he was going to
catch. He was after a trophy. Something he could tack up
on his wall with an infinite satisfaction. But the catch
wasn't the reward he was after. Not even close.

"I'll be waiting," D'Angelo promised. "Your call."

A cold linear sense of purpose shivered through Xander
the way the air-conditioning hadn't been able to. Just a few
short steps left to take. To be sure. This one he couldn't let
escape because he'd taken shortcuts. And the payoff would
be sweet revenge.

And thinking of sweet derailed his train of thought.

"Why didn't you tell me Mel Parrish was a woman?"

There was a pause, then D'Angelo gave a nonplussed
laugh. "I didn't think it would make a difference. Does it?"

Xander drew up a mental picture of Mel Parrish in the enticingly curved flight suit, of her boldly angular face, flashing dark eyes and sassy mouth. And that untamed mass of red hair. He shut his eyes, canceling out the image.

"No, of course not."

Kyle D'Angelo chuckled. "She's hot—she must be, to rattle a monk like you."

How could D'Angelo tell he was rattled from that one concise sentence? But then Kyle knew him better than he knew himself. And, unfortunately, he was right. Xander tightened down the screws on the press of his emotions and vowed, "It won't matter."

"I'm sure it won't. Not with that gift you've got."

Because it sounded like some kind of unpleasant disease, Xander frowned. "What gift is that?"

"You have an amazing gift of blankness, my friend. Slick. Smooth. Nonabsorbing. Nothing gets to you with your nonstick coating. It just slides right off. I don't know if I envy that or not. It makes you kind of a scary guy."

Xander tried to laugh it off but couldn't. Was that what he was? Was that what he'd become?

"Thanks a hell of a lot, Kyle."

And because D'Angelo knew him so well, he caught the hint of something unexpected behind that mocking sentiment. He'd somehow managed to wound his usually stoic friend.

"It was a compliment. I didn't mean to hurt your feelings."

"No danger of that since apparently I don't have any."

He could picture D'Angelo's grin at having provoked the cynical response. And his own dark mood gave a notch as he managed a small smile.

"Thought you might have lost your sense of humor there for a minute."

"Misplaced it, perhaps." He pinched the bridge of his nose to stave off the tension headache that was building from a distant rumbling to fearsome thunderheads. "I had to pack light for this trip. It wasn't a must-have item."

"Don't leave home without it, bud. It's the all-purpose Rx." Predictably, Kyle shifted into life counselor mode to offer his one prescription for everything. "When was the last time you kicked your shoes off?"

He wiggled his bare toes. "They're off right now."

"That's not what I mean and you know it. You need to get a life, bud. All work and no play."

"Makes Xander a scary guy. I know."

"And I know the remedy. Leave everything to Dr. D'Angelo. What say we just take the weekend off. Zip up to Colorado to your mom's condo. Hit the clubs, jump in a hot tub with some lonely lovelies, cigars and a fifth of your choice and enjoy a total hedonistic orgy. How does that sound?"

"Like we were frat boys again." He was smiling, imagining it. Kyle drew lonely ladies and hedonistic good times like a bacchanalian magnet.

"Tell me you're not tempted."

Tempted, yes. Because he couldn't remember the last time he had taken a break. He'd been wound so tight for so long, he wasn't sure he could loosen up the notch it would take to be a suitable companion for fun. Not because he didn't need it, but because he didn't deserve it. Especially now.

"I'll have to pass," he said softly, without true regret. "Maybe when this is over."

He heard Kyle's resigned sigh, knowing his friend hadn't really expected any other answer. "It's never over with you."

"If this pans out, it will be."

Then maybe he could take a breather. Now, it was hard to even think of having a good time when he knew others didn't have the luxury. For some, there were no breaks, no willing ladies, no hot tubs. That's why he had to work harder and stay focused. Kyle may not like it, but he did understand it. Because he knew why his friend was a scary guy.

"Keep in touch, bud. Be careful. We'll nail this one down for you. Anything I can do, anything, you let me know."

A huge knot of gratitude interfered with his immediate response. When he was able to give it, the words came out all rough and raw. "I appreciate it, Kyle. More than you know."

Uncomfortable with the thought of his sincerity, D'Angelo shifted back to a light touch. "So Mel Parrish is a woman. And she's hot. No wonder you're so grouchy. If I were you, I'd be thinking about on-the-job perks."

"Goodbye, Kyle."

He was smiling as he flipped the phone shut. Then his mouth narrowed into a thin, hard line. Mel Parrish wasn't a perk. She was a puzzle piece. And finding out where she fit in was his reason for sitting alone in a hotel room in Reno.

A monk. A surprisingly apt description. There was a time when he'd never have spent a night in a hotel room alone with only work and late-night television for company. But not being alone didn't necessarily mean not being lonely. Surrounding himself with a crowd only brought that home with a more painful clarity. So he took a step back from that party-hardy set who had no cares, no worries, no

real depth of purpose. All those who had once courted him
for his name, his contacts and his fortune, the men who
wanted him to buy them drinks and invest in their projects,
the women who wanted to hang on his arm to get their pictures in the entertainment news. All those frivolous, fun
people who had abandoned him at that first dark whisper
of scandal. He'd didn't miss them. He didn't need their shallow company. For what he was doing, the isolation served
him best. It kept him lean, mean and dangerously determined. But it made for long, lonely nights.

Perhaps that was why Mel Parrish left him shaken, not
stirred.

Business casual or escort service.

He grinned wide at the brazenness of that remark.
Hooker clothes couldn't look more enticing than that one-
piece zippered distraction. Every curve seemed shaped to
fit his hands. And the suddenly damp state of his palms
made him aware of just how long he'd been celibate. Too
long to remember the circumstance or participant. He told
himself that was the reason for his unwise attraction. But
he knew he was lying. It was the woman, herself not his
reclusive state. It was her eyes, that bold-as-brass-tacks
stare that let him know in unblinking terms that he was being an ass. No one, other than Kyle, had dared do that for
a very long time. And damned if it didn't impress him.

A brisk slap of realization startled him from his half
smile and simmering musings. What was he thinking?

Back to business. Time was short and he had work to do.

Beneath the official insurance file was a thin folder that
held the pain of his past. It contained three meager docu-
ments—a fire investigation, an arrest report and a trial

transcript. The impossibly weak foundation upon which he'd been struggling to erect the means to escape his shame.

He didn't want to be impressed by Mel Parrish.

He wanted to put her and her family in prison.

Chapter 3

"Is this better?"

She stood in the hall outside his room, her arrogant pose daring him to make some comment about the way she was dressed. Impossible. His tongue had adhered to the roof of his mouth.

She'd decided to blend both professional and the oldest profession into a look that was in-your-face tough and tempting. Her frizz of red hair was in a ponytail back beneath a ball cap to accentuate the no-nonsense angles of her face warmed by only a trace of makeup. A conservative black jacket that would have been right at home in a realty seminar framed the body that her flight suit had only hinted at. The tiny shirt she wore beneath it with its cutesy cartoon character motif and preteen proportions left acres of Mel Parrish bare. The long tanned line of her

throat led his gaze downward to plunge dangerously into
a careless offer of cleavage. Then that teensy scrap of snug
knit defining the hills and valleys of her breasts the way a
man's hands might above an expanse of taut, toned middle.
The sassy wink of jewel-pierced belly button snagged his
attention long enough for him to catch a shallow breath before being confronted with the low scoop of her jeans just
barely hanging on her hipbones. The negligent crisscross
of a studded belt was slung atop denim-skinned legs. In his
fantasy, she would be wearing stiletto heels instead of
clunky work boots, but those almost absurd contrasts
worked upon his no-longer-monkish libido. Kyle's assessment of "hot" didn't even come close to the scorch of her
boldly flaunted sexuality. And what made the whole package beyond hot was the challenging bristle of look-don't-
touch she exuded.

He had to remind himself to exhale.

"Fine." His rough growl rumbled across the agitation he
refused to betray. Mel Parrish would never know how
much his palms itched to skim around the warm curve of
her waist, to pull her up tight against contours not quite so
thrilled with his self-denying celibacy. "I'm ready."

An incredible understatement.

The elevator grew more crowded as they picked up pas-
sengers on each floor. Crushed up next to her, Xander found
his stare discreetly dipping down into the shadowed crevice
between his bodyguard's breasts. And on the other side of
her, the luggage handler was enjoying that same lush scenery with a bit less care. Mel's elbow flashed back, jabbing
the poor fellow just above the belt, making him suck a pain-
filled breath as she murmured a mild "Excuse me."

Xander's gaze jumped front and center, missing the way hers cut to him suspiciously. Then her lids lowered slightly as she indulged in an appreciative sweep of her own.

Some men were made to wear expensive suits. Xander Caufield had the strong, tailored physique and coldly superior attitude to carry off the elitist look to perfection. But in that brief second, when she caught him staring unashamedly down her neckline, there was nothing remotely civilized about him. That dangerous edge of desire making a raw slash across his reserve had her shivering in response. And she thought once again about taking that bounce on the taut bedcovers beneath him.

What grew taut between them during the long day was the silence. After the contents of his case had been delivered to the exhibit floor during the chaos of booth setups, they headed to California for another pickup. They didn't speak. Xander took his seat in back and left the flying to Mel, apparently content to place himself in her hands. A delightful notion that kept her busy for most of the flight imagining just how one might go about peeling off his prickly protective layers to get to the good stuff inside. His posture never relaxed, not once on the trip there or back, and that made her nervous, wondering if there really was some sort of danger involved in what he was doing. She was very aware of the pistol pressing against the small of her back, and though well versed in its use, she wasn't eager to pull it in the heat of confrontation.

Stepping from the sear of late-afternoon heat into the near brain-freeze chill of hotel air-conditioning, Mel was thinking about the lunch she didn't have and whether or not it would be appropriate to ask her client if he wanted to join her at the hotel's Mexican restaurant for some off-the-clock tequila and spicy food. Perhaps if they were forced to sit across from each other like civilized human beings, they would have to think up some polite conversation to fill the time. Something that didn't have to do with her wardrobe or the crisp hotel bedspread. Not sure what other topics were up for grabs, she got into the elevator behind him and started mentally rehearsing. The car was going down one before heading up to the tenth floor. Xander had opted to take it rather than wait for the other elevators to return from the double digit floors. Just as the doors began to close, a trio of multiple-pierced punks slipped into the car with them with polite murmurs of "Excuse me," and quietly waited behind them. Until the doors opened.

A series of subterranean tunnels ran beneath the hotel, offering shopping at touristy and exclusive shops. At four-thirty, when most guests were preoccupied by dinner alternatives, they offered a very quiet and unpopulated spot away from the rush of the upper floors. Away from everything, Mel realized a second too late when she saw two more toughs loitering just outside the doors. As she reached for the Close button, she sensed movement behind them.

Sudden, hard shoves propelled both of them out of the elevator car. One of the punks gripped Mel by the lapels of her jacket, swinging her around and dragging her quickly out of the open area into one of the empty side halls. Xander followed stiffly, urged by a glitter of steel nudged up under his chin.

"We want what's in your pockets and in the case," growled the Mohawk-wearing fellow holding Mel. Then his voice lowered and its softness was somehow more threatening. "And maybe if you cooperate, that's all we'll want."

Cursing her carelessness, Mel assessed their situation. A security camera was aimed down the hallway, but its lens was spray painted over. There was no foot traffic. Obviously, their assailants had planned for this meeting a lot better than she had. They were pushed back against one of the walls. Cutting a quick glance at Xander, she was impressed by his stoic expression. As she prayed there would be no reckless heroics to get them killed, those hopes were dashed when he caught her look. His expression was fearless. Slowly, grimly, he smiled.

"I'm reaching for my wallet," he told the trio surrounding him as he dipped in his trouser pocket. Their greedy attention focused on those fat leather folds and not him, tracking the wallet as it fell to the floor between them. As they went after it, he swung the case, catching the one with the knife in the temple, dropping him like a rock. A vicious upward arc took the next one in the face, pulping his nose and sending him reeling back with a howl of pained surprise.

Figuring it was time to follow her client's lead, Mel grabbed for her gun. Mohawk read the move and intercepted it, twisting her wrist, wrenching it up behind her back. She didn't waste time struggling. He was obviously stronger. Instead, she stomped down on his instep and applied her other elbow to his groin. Suddenly freed, she spilled onto the floor on hands and knees. Before she could gain any momentum on the slick tiles, large hands grabbed her about the waist, yanking her up. She kicked the man in front of her, taking him in the kneecap. As he crumpled, she drove back with her elbows, inflicting as much damage as she could. And that's when her captor swung her around and the side of her head met with one of the support pillars.

Darkness swamped over her in a huge, sickening wave as she was hauled back up to her feet. She got a blurry glimpse of Xander dropping the case, his hands spreading wide in presumed surrender. His stare touched on the blood streaming down the side of her face, on the hands holding her, one by the throat and one groping roughly in search of her weapon. And she realized their attackers were wrong to think the danger was from her gun.

He moved so fast and purposefully they had no time to react. Gripping the knife-wielding hand, dodging its lethal thrust, he dropped his elbow down at the base of the man's skull. A knee to the face as he was falling took him completely out of the picture. Even as Xander shoved away from the first man, he was intent upon the next, using combined strikes from the back of his fist and elbow followed by a hard upward drive with the heel of his other hand to dispatch thug number two.

Mel had never seen anything like him. She was familiar with bar brawls and self-defense but not this skilled form of controlled attack. He didn't fight using a fisted punch but rather with fierce hard strikes, using every surface of his body with explosive aggressive force—knees, elbows, the flat of his forearms, even his head, to batter his assailants into submission. Without hesitation, without mercy. Until a roar from Mohawk checked him.

"Enough!"

The blade pressed to Mel's throat effectively stilled Xander's unexpected threat. He took a submissive stance, his hard glare riveted to the others as he issued a quiet promise.

"Cut her and I'll end you."

The deadly force behind that delivery gave Mohawk an instant of hesitation. Just enough for Mel to act in her own defense. She gripped his thumb, twisting it back until his fingers opened and the knife dropped. As she backed out of his slackened hold, she pulled her pistol free and jammed it into his kidney.

"Think about it!" Mel said.

He froze, apparently thinking hard.

"Run."

He didn't have to think twice about that one. He bolted and the rest of his group scrambled after him.

The pistol in her hand wavered wildly. The floor, walls and ceiling began a slow, determined roll. Mel was dimly aware of a firm grip divesting her of the gun, curling about her waist to ease her fall into blackness. After that, it was just dizzying snatches. The sight of an oxygen mask coming down from a backdrop of flashing lights. Of Xander's immobile features filling her field of vision, a dark angel at her side. His small, tight smile of reassurance and the warm chafe of his hands over one of hers. And the gleam of metal from the courier case in his lap flaring bright as passing streetlights reflected off it. Then darkness, cool and complete.

They swarmed the E.R. like soldiers storming the battlements. Her family, her friends, pushing him out of the way. He shouldn't have resented surrendering his seat at her bedside. And he wondered why he did.

He'd been sitting on the hard metal chair for the past four hours while emergency staff plugged her in and took her vitals. He acted as if he belonged there and after a while, they stopped questioning his right to be. He didn't interfere with them, content to remain a silent sentinel, her hand within the curl of his fingers, his attention riveted to her pale features. All the alarm and fear that hadn't surfaced while confronting the thugs in the hotel whispered through him now as he kept an anxious eye on the monitors and waited for her to wake up—this gutsy woman who would risk her life for him. The fact that she was well paid to do so never quite entered the equation.

They wheeled her out briefly to get a CT scan. While he sat alone behind the curtained walls, with sounds of weeping and suffering on either side of him, he noticed with an odd detachment the blood splashed on his shirtfront and hands. He stared at the dark patterns for a long moment before finally getting up to wash them off in the small sink. That's when his hands started shaking, tremors spreading until they raced all the way to the soles of his no-longer-spotless shoes. Delayed shock. A trickle-down of adrenaline. That's all it was. His eyes squeezed tight. She could have died right then, right there, protecting his lie.

"Mel?"

Xander scooped a palmful of water and dashed it on his face. Using the sleeve of his ruined jacket to towel it dry, he turned to the anxious man staring at the empty bed in horror.

"She's getting tests done."

Relief dropped the older man to the chair Xander had vacated. He sat sucking air, his face pale as the lightweight cotton blanket folded at the end of the bed.

"I'm Xander Caufield."

Dazed eyes lifted to register his presence. "Charley Parrish. Mel's my niece. Is she all right? What happened?"

Before he could begin, there was a ruckus in the hall. Six men smelling of smoke and hard work pushed their way past the curtain, followed by a harried nurse. They all talked at once, addressing Charley Parrish as if he had the answers. No one paid Xander the least bit of attention.

Then Mel's welcome voice intruded. "Hey, you guys mind keeping it down. There are sick people in here."

They parted to allow room for the gurney carrying a pale but smiling Mel Parrish, then quickly closed ranks about her bed. Leaving Xander on the outside.

"They find anything in that empty head of yours?"

"What's the other guy look like?"

"Like we don't have enough to do without worrying about your sorry butt. Hey, Charley. How ya doing?"

"That was one helluva scare you gave us when we heard it on the scanner, One Night."

"Give her room to breathe, fellas."

Xander observed them, these big, gruff men all jockeying for the chance to clutch her hand within their dirty paws while she looked up at them with obvious affection. The scene acted strangely upon him. These were the ones who loved her and were loved in return. Hearing she was in trouble, they'd dropped everything to come running. Though they joked and grumbled about the inconvenience, the edge of worried concern was etched in each rugged face. That told him more about Mel Parrish than any amount of research he could have gathered.

"Hey, is this where the party is?"

"Sir, gentlemen, you can't all go in there!"

"Hey, One Night. Whatcha doing on that bed all by yourself? Want some company?"

"Why? Do you have a good-looking friend?"

Laughter. Warm and rich with relief as more of the men shouldered their way into the small sterile space. Crowding Xander—with his bloodstained clothes and unfamiliar face—out. He lingered a moment longer, absorbing the sight of her surrounded by her fiercely protective posse of devoted comrades, her smile wide and reckless, her eyes shiny with emotion. Then he picked up his case and backed away unnoticed.

By all but one.

Chapter 4

It was her worst hangover squared.

Moving woke an *Anvil Chorus* between her temples punctuated by the cannons from the *1812 Overture*. Every inch of her ached. She had no business crawling out of bed, except the business she had to take care of. She'd used all her persuasive powers on the physician at the E.R. to agree to let her go home without an overnight stay.

Now, to find out if she still had a job.

After shaking a few more pain relievers into her hand and swallowing them dry, she gathered the courage to knock.

He'd saved her butt the night before. There was no way around that. Her mistakes had almost gotten them both killed. If she had a scrap of self-respect, she'd make her apologies and gracefully resign. But she needed the paycheck.

Desperately. And now she had the E.R. bill hanging over her head, bouncing behind her aching eyes like a bad check.

He'd done more than come to her rescue. That's what chafed her emotions raw. He'd stayed with her. Though she'd been drifting in and out, the only constant she could recall was his presence. And she'd clung to it and the firm press of his hand. In the ambulance, in the E.R., he'd stuck by her, offering up a small smile of encouragement as she lay helpless. She hadn't had the chance to thank him. And he hadn't told her goodbye. She'd tried to find him through the thick forest of her friends but he was gone. And even though she'd been surrounded by noisy familiarity, she'd felt suddenly alone.

The door opened and they stood face-to-face.

A rush of complex feelings had Mel tongue-tied and awkward. What did you say to a man who'd saved your life and babysat you through a trauma unit? What did you say when your heart was abruptly hammering hard and fast with a press of emotions that gratitude couldn't come close to explaining? The urge to fling her arms about his neck and steam the stiffness from his lips with her kiss had her trembling in an effort at restraint.

His brusque attitude saved her from that mistake.

"I need to make another pickup from the seller in California. He's gotten an offer for the rest of his collection and the buyer wants a look at it first."

He stepped back from the door and went to get his coat. Mel blinked, totally off balance. No inquiry as to her health. No sign of concern whatsoever. After cradling her hand and wearing her blood on his designer clothes, he was back to all business as if they'd never shared… What? What had they shared? What was she trying to make out of it? She cleared her throat gruffly and squared her stance, trying to appear competent and in control while her careening thoughts and emotions pinballed inside her.

"I got a clean bill to fly."

He didn't even glance around. "I assumed as much or you wouldn't be here."

I'm fine. Thank you for asking.

He shrugged into his suit jacket, grabbed up his case and brushed by her without a glance. Expressing a sigh, Mel followed. And she followed the way he moved with a new appreciation. Xander Caufield was full of surprises.

Once closed in the elevator together, they stood shoulder to shoulder, both intently watching the floor numbers count down. Might as well get it over with.

"Thank you."

No shift in expression betrayed that he'd heard her. Just when she was about to swallow down her pride to say more, she felt the brush of his fingertips against hers. Then the warm, firm squeeze of his hand. That was it.

Enough said. She smiled faintly to herself as the doors opened to the lobby.

The fact that he chose to sit up front with her said more. She hoped it wasn't because he was afraid he'd have to be there to catch her if she decided to pass out.

Once they were in the air and cruising, she glanced over at his immobile profile. When she lifted up the edge of his jacket, he turned to her in what was almost alarm.

"Just wondering where you kept the superhero suit."

"What?"

"I haven't seen moves like yours outside of an afternoon adventure matinee."

A slight smile but no response. She prompted him with a lift of her brows.

"Private school."

It was her turn to look confused.

"I was that skinny, sensitive, geeky kid with glasses who used to get beaten up every morning for his café latte money. I was Alex Caufield III back then and I used to hide in the janitor's closet until after the final bell so I could sneak into my seat without a bloody nose. There was no dignity in it but it was a lot less painful."

"So your folks enrolled you in martial arts classes?"

"No. My mother didn't believe violence was a solution to any problem. So I used my café latte money to pay our Korean gardener to teach me how to kick the crap out of anyone who got in my face. Classes are for earning trophies. Street fighting is to keep your glasses from getting broken."

"And now no one gets in your face," she concluded, impressed but not wanting to show it.

A small smug smile. No, she supposed they didn't.

"So why hire me when you can do your own crap kicking?"

"Company policy. Liability purposes." Catching her thoughtful look, he turned his attention to the scenery, ending the exchange of more words than they'd totaled for the past two days. She reassessed him with a leisurely look. A street fighter in Armani. An enticing contradiction.

They traveled in silence for a time until he broke it with a soft oath. She followed his stare downward and understood his horror. They were approaching the fire zone.

It was like flying over hell.

A crackle of static on the radio had Mel quickly adjusting the frequency. And what she managed to pick up chilled her.

"Firefighter down. Requests emergency extraction."

The signal was weak and breaking up. She put on her headphones to filter out the copter noise, but still the message was fragmented. She waited, breath suspended.

"Come on. Somebody answer."

"What is it?"

Alerted by her tone and tense posture, Xander pulled the earphone away so she could hear his urgent question. The look she gave him was stark with dismay.

"One of our guys is down. He got cut off from his crew by a sudden backfire. He's injured. I don't know how bad."

"He's down there?" Xander nodded to the inferno below.

"Yes."

"Isn't someone going in for him?"

"I don't think his call got out."

He followed her anxious attempts to contact the stranded firefighter who wasn't answering. She put out a call to any nearby aircraft, but the closest was too far away to do the injured man any good. She cursed low and passionately. The nose of the copter dipped and they swooped down to skim the burning treetops. The heat was sudden and intense. Struggling to see through the thick haze of smoke, Xander finally called out, "There he is."

The situation was a worst-case scenario. They could see the single figure, prostrate on the ground with the fury of the beast rushing toward him. Mel tried the radio again. No answer.

"There's no place for me to set down and he can't hook himself up to a harness."

"I'll go down."

She must not have heard him right. "What?"

"I'll go down after him."

She stared at him, flabbergasted. "Are you crazy?"

He never even blinked. "You've got a hoist back there, right? I'll go down after him and you bring us both back up."

He made it sound so simple. Her heart started beating fast and furious. "You have no idea how dangerous—"

"I've been rock climbing and base jumping since I was fifteen. I know how to rappel. Does that man have the time it'll take for you to check my credentials?" His voice lowered, becoming rough, soft and persuasive. "Mel, you're going to have to trust me. I know what I'm doing. And I'm going to have to trust you to pull me out of there before both of us are barbecue."

She continued to stare at him, expression frozen, eyes huge. Finally he unhooked his straps and stood. "I'm going to go rig up. You get in as close as you can. It doesn't look like we've got much of a window of opportunity."

She gripped his wrist, holding hard, needing him to understand the gravity of his situation. "I don't have any safety equipment on board. Once you're outside, I can't help you."

He covered her hand with his, pressing hard. "I'll let you know when I'm ready."

She watched him work his way to the back, swaying with the rock of the Ranger as the rising heat created a vicious turbulence. She would have cursed again but her heart had bobbed up into her throat, choking her with desperate emotion.

What kind of man dropped into hell in his shirtsleeves for someone he didn't even know?

The quick and competent way he fastened up the harness said he knew what he was doing. His expression was grimly focused. If he was afraid, she couldn't tell. There was no hesitation in his movements. She could have been looking at one of the seasoned hotshots about to fly like an eagle. Except he was plunging into a furnace with no oxygen and no fire suit.

"Here."

He caught the bandanna she tossed back.

"Hold your breath," she warned. She'd be holding hers. "I'm giving you thirty seconds and then you're coming up with or without him. Understand?"

He nodded, not looking at her as he uncapped one of the bottled waters in the back, pouring it into the cloth square then over his head to wet his hair and face. Then he fixed her anxious gaze with his own steady one and told her, "Don't let me fry."

She tried to answer but couldn't form the words.

He tied the soaked bandanna over his nose and mouth and opened the door. The stench of smoke poured in. He swung the hoist out and locked the cable onto his harness. Then, with one long look at her, he gave a thumbs-up, stepped out into the hazy air and was gone.

There was no time to worry about him. She had her hands full keeping the Ranger at a low steady hover just above the trees. She began to count. *One thousand one. One thousand two.* She couldn't see him as he was directly below the belly of her ship, but she could see the flames chewing across her memory. And she could hear the screams, pleading for rescue from the horrible reaches of her past. *One thousand seventeen. One thousand eighteen.* She tried not to think about the poisonous gases, the heat, the flames. *One thousand twenty-nine. One thousand thirty. Ready or not.*

She activated the hoist, her breath still suspended as she swiveled in her seat to watch the empty doorway.

She's right. I'm crazy.

Sure, he'd done bungee jumping and rappelling. But not into a raging volcano. And the difference was searingly apparent as he sang down the line into the fire. He took a deep breath—the last he could safely pull until he was back in the helicopter—and plunged to the floor of hell.

One thousand three. One thousand four.

The heat hit like a closed fist, the waves of it so intense the water and instant sweat beading up his face and neck sizzled. Walls of flame pressed in on all sides. He could hear the sap popping in the firs as it boiled. Tongues of fire raced across the dry grasses under his feet, licking at the still figure stretched out on the ground. His vision blurred behind the scorch of smoke as he bent over the unconscious man. From the corner of his eye, he saw something fall and reached without thinking to catch a limb as big around as his forearm, deflecting if before it struck the downed firefighter. He could smell the cooked flesh on his palms before the pain actually registered. Then he gasped and; immediately, was coughing, choking, reeling.

One thousand twelve. One thousand thirteen.

He couldn't draw a breath. His nose, his throat, his lungs burned with a raw, tearing agony. Dropping down onto elbows and knees, he swayed, struggling not to succumb. Seconds. He only had seconds to secure the other man's safety.

One thousand twenty. One thousand twenty-one.

He crouched over the firefighter, wincing as he grabbed onto his slack weight and dragged him up into a seated position. Buffeted by dizziness and the relentless pounding waves of heat, he banded the man's chest and locked his arms about him.

One thousand twenty-seven.

Burning embers lit on the back of his neck. He shook his head but couldn't knock them off. Not without letting go. He gritted his teeth. *Come on, Mel! Get me out of here!*

And then the line pulled taut, dragging him and his limp cargo up and off their feet, snatching them up through the thick plumes of blackness. He was barely aware of them stopping. Of his feet groping for the open doorway. Of swinging his heavy burden inside. Of collapsing, crawling the last few feet and rolling onto his back to suck the first sweet taste of air.

At the controls, Mel shouted back, "Alex, are you in?"

Then his hoarse reply. "Go."

Mel headed back to Reno, not daring to turn around until they touched down on tarmac where the ambulance waited by the Parrish hangar. She threw out of her belts and hurried back to where Xander sat on the floor beside the still firefighter, one hand clutching the other's motionless fingers, the other rubbing at his own eyes. He glanced up when Mel touched the back of his dark head. His face was a mess of black soot smeared by runnels from bloodshot eyes. From out of it, his wide smile was a sudden shock of white. Relief and something bigger, something massive, plugged up in her chest.

"We got him, Mel."

Her own smile wobbled. "Yes, we did."

The paramedics were quick to secure the young fire-fighter, Teddy Greenbaum, to a stretcher. They had Xander breathe through an oxygen mask until he could suck air without spasms of coughing. He let them take his vitals then declined further attention with a gruff "I'm fine," and a promise that he'd check in with them if he had any problems.

Then Teddy Greenbaum, who'd been scant minutes from beyond help, was whisked away to the hospital.

"Come on," Mel coaxed the slumping figure of Xander Caufield. "I'll stand you to a cold one."

Groaning, he slid off the chopper step onto his feet and took a reeling pitch to the right.

"Whoa. I gotcha."

Mel slipped in under his arm and let him lean on her while he gathered his bearings then steered him toward the hangar. Acting without thinking, she sat him down in her swivel desk chair, stuck an opened longneck in his hand and went for the first-aid kit in the small bathroom. She came back to find him hunched over, untouched beer dangling between his knees. She tipped his head back with the cup of her palm beneath his chin. His sore eyes were flat with fatigue as they fixed upon hers. Slowly, very gently, she began to clean off his face with the wet towel she'd brought for that purpose. His eyes closed as she uncovered more of his splendid features with each determined swipe. Beautifully masculine lines. Irresistible. She bent, touching her mouth to his. He tasted like dry ash on the outside. Sweet, so sweet inside. When she lifted away, his eyes were still shut, his breath coming softly, shallowly between the slight part of his lips. With her hand on the back of his head, she had him tuck his chin so she could attend the singed nape of his neck while her fingers meshed and kneaded his dirty hair. All the while a curious fullness kept building around her heart.

Crouching between the spread of his knees, Mel took the beer from him and had a long drink of it before setting it aside. She took up his hands, again, her touch so very tender, examining the blistered palms.

"There's no easy way to do this, Alex."

He braced at the quiet warning.

At the first touch of the ointment to the raw skin on his hand, white-hot pain ripped along every nerve ending, slashing, sharp, gnawing, right-to-the-bone agony that had his heels clattering a helpless staccato on the cement floor. Just when he thought his teeth were gritting with enough force to crack molars, she stopped and blew slowly over the aggrieved surface to win some small degree of relief. She looked up at him and he managed a tight smile as he offered up the other hand the way he might to a meat grinder. By the time she was done, he was panting and blinking hard. But still, that small slight smile.

"You could have told me it would sting a bit," he chided, then was dismayed when the brightness shimmering in her eyes dissolved in a blink, tracing down her cheeks in quick-silver trails. Her palms pressed flat to his chest, moving up and down in a restless motion before fisting in his soiled shirt. She leaned into him, butting her head against him between those clenched hands. And she began to tremble.

With his hands all gooey and trapped in a swaddling of gauze, he was at a loss to do more than trap her quaking shoulders between the press of his elbows. Resting his cheek against the soft riot of her hair, he closed his eyes and rode out her silent weeping without a word.

"Mel?"

The sound of her uncle's worried voice had her pulling back, pulling herself together with quick, self-preserving practice. She stood away from Xander Caufield, away from the sudden confusion of feelings that had her lost and seeking comfort from the embrace of this near stranger, who had managed, for a brief moment, to hold her fears at bay.

"I passed an ambulance. What's going on?" Charley's gaze cut between the careful opaque of her expression to that of her rumpled and worse-for-wear client. "Everything all right here?"

"A little unscheduled stop to pick up a passenger. I'll explain it to you later, Charley."

Sensing there were volumes she wasn't saying, Charley simply nodded. He was too used to the complexities behind his niece's brusque manner to push for more than she was ready to give.

"We're running late for a pickup," she continued so he wouldn't have time to press for additional information. She needed time to sort it out, to suppress her reactions, and she didn't want to risk spilling any more pieces of her soul in front of Xander. He'd seen more than she was comfortable with already.

More than he was comfortable with, if she read his impenetrable facade correctly. He gave nothing away when she glanced at him.

"Are you up for another trip?"

"As long as there are no more unscheduled stops. I want to shower and change first. I'm rather...unpresentable."

She took in the whole of him, the smudges of ash, the suit that was far beyond the help of any dry cleaner, the stink of smoke and sweat. And nothing had looked more attractive, more appealing, than this rumpled version of Xander Caufield.

"I'll bring the car around," she managed in a tight little voice, using that excuse to run from the confusion of her heart.

Xander met Charley Parrish's curious stare unflinchingly. Finally the other man fidgeted and came out with it.

"Mel told me what you did the other night. I never got the chance to thank you at the hospital." He held up a hand before Xander could brush off his gratitude. "That girl and my daughter are the only things that mean a damn to me. They're my life. I just wanted you to know that, so when I say thank-you, you'll know it's more than just words."

Because there was no way to respond to that, Xander simply nodded.

Charley cleared his throat awkwardly. "My daughter Karen wanted a chance to thank you, too. She's got a private gallery showing over in Tahoe tomorrow night and asked me to extend you an invite. I don't know if you're interested in that kind of thing or have the time for it. Mel can bring you."

"Bring him where?"

"To Karen's showing tomorrow night."

Mel's wary glare bored into her uncle's, chastening him for his bumbling attempt at matchmaking. "I'm sure Mr. Caufield has better things—"

"No, actually I don't," Xander cut in. "It would be a nice distraction from room service and pay-TV." He paused then added silkily, "If you don't mind."

"No trouble at all." She checked her watch. "We've got about forty-five minutes to get in the air."

Nodding to Charley, Xander followed Mel out to her battered Jeep. After climbing in, in deference to her tense mood, he said, "Don't feel obligated. If you have other plans—" He let that drift off.

She glanced at him. Other plans? Plans better than spending an off-the-clock evening with him? *Let me check my calendar?* Her smile was fierce. "If I minded, I would have said so. Buckle up."

The Jeep jerked forward, giving Xander scant time to grab on. He continued to study the tight set of her jaw and the rigid line of her shoulders. She minded plenty. But she was taking him where he needed to go.

Play the role. Remember the part. And try not to look forward to it quite so much.

Chapter 5

A shower and a change of clothes. Easy to say, harder to execute with the way pain was pulsing up from his fingertips. He glanced at Mel Parrish, who was gazing out the window of his hotel room toward the pool area ten floors below. What would she say if he were to ask if she'd mind helping him undress, suds up and towel dry? If she minded following up on that tease of a kiss that had sucked the oxygen from his lungs as effectively as the fire? Would she give him that cool, assessing stare and say no problem?

Maybe she would.

"I'll be just a minute."

He had started for the bathroom when she said his name. She called him Alex. No one had called him that for longer than he could remember. Except his parents, who would always see him as the awkward Alex rather than the coldly confident Xander he'd worked so hard to cultivate. He didn't correct her. He liked the way she pronounced it, all soft instead of the crisp-cut syllables of his new persona.

"Here. I brought these for you to use."

He stared at the plastic bags and rubber bands, not understanding.

"Put them over your hands to keep the dressings dry. Unless you want me to reapply the salve."

The threat made him grimace. "No, thanks. And thanks."

She released a shaky breath after the bathroom door closed and she heard the shower turn on full blast. She'd been about to say, *Let me know if you need any help.* Help to do what, exactly? She glanced restlessly at the closed door, angrily denying that what she wanted was to help herself to her quixotic client. She paced, thoughts prowling aggressively, until the water shut off and a long silence followed. Finally, he emerged, dressed in dark slacks with his crisp white shirt unbuttoned, his black hair slicked back and gleaming wetly. He struggled for a moment with a bottle then extended it to her in frustration.

"I can't get this."

She took the bottle, popped the plastic childproof top and shook out four of the pain relievers. He reached for them, hand unsteady, and was quick to swallow them. Observing the pinch of pain about his mouth and eyes, she asked, "Are you sure you don't need a prescription, something with a little more kick?"

"No, this is fine."

But he was far from fine and not happy that she knew it. Intuiting that he wouldn't ask for further assistance short of dialing 9-1-1, she relieved him of the embarrassment of asking by stepping up closer and efficiently buttoned his shirt over the temptation of a truly amazing chest while he stood still and silent. Before he could object, she unbuckled his pants and tucked the shirttails in with a brisk efficiency. As he stared down at her, not breathing, she zipped him back up and impersonally patted his taut middle.

"There. The rest shouldn't be difficult for you."

What was difficult was expelling his breath in a steady stream.

Their second attempt at a flight to California went smoothly. Xander sat in the back, staring moodily out the window on the way there and slept with what appeared to be a fierce concentration on the way back. She waited in the lobby while he had the contents of his case placed in a hotel safe-deposit box and it was there he said a clipped good-night to her. As he turned away, she snagged him with that quiet call of his name.

"Business casual."

"What?"

"Dress for tomorrow night. Unless you'd prefer escort service."

At his slight smile when he caught the reference, she added, "Drive or fly?"

"I'll meet you there. I'm looking up a friend for drinks afterward."

Her features remained carefully neutral. "Fine. Seven." She told him the address. He didn't write it down. Then, with a nod and the small curve of his smile, he disappeared into the mob on the casino floor.

* * *

A collection of Tahoe's elite gathered in the multilevel gallery in the silent shadow of the off-season ski runs to nibble on canapés, sip fairly decent champagne and stroll amongst Karen Parrish's paintings, admiring and making small talk. Mel could spend hours gazing at her cousin's ethereal landscapes, but after the first five minutes, her tolerance for chitchat was expended. The only things that made it bearable were the sounds of her cousin's laughter and the man she pretended not to be watching for.

"You just missed Quinn. He could only stay for a minute."

Mel smiled tightly, forgiving her cousin for the softening of her voice and heart. And head. Karen was usually so much smarter. But she'd always had an unrequited yearning where the Texas playboy was concerned. "Probably just as well considering civil conversation is out of the question between us."

"Then what is between you?"

Mel was busy sifting through the new arrivals and missed the edge to the question. "A good right hook, if I had my way. Naylor's a pain in the behind. Always was. Always will be."

Karen relaxed, tracking her younger relative's focus to the door.

"Client, huh?"

Mel refused to respond to her cousin's teasing. "He just mentioned he'd stop by. It's no big deal. He's got plans."

Plans involving someone of unspecified gender.

"So Mr. No Big Deal rates this little old thing you're wearing? I haven't seen you in nylons since your junior prom."

"Well, I haven't met anyone worth shaving my legs for."

"And this one is?"

She didn't have to answer. For the briefest instant, the look of potential heartache was all over her face. "Probably not. Well…maybe. Oh, Karen, he's…"

"Wow," her cousin sighed.

"Exactly." Then Mel noticed Karen was staring pointedly and followed her gaze.

Alexander Caufield quite simply stole her breath away.

He'd dressed down in black jeans and T-shirt under an expensive charcoal-colored jacket. And black high-top tennis shoes, the laces dangling with a boyish appeal. His idea of casual was calculated enough for a photo shoot. He paused at the entrance to the gallery, scanning the crowd without hurry.

"Go get him, Mel. This one I want to meet."

Her rush across the room was anything but unhurried. The way his gaze darkened when it lit upon her caused her to skid and stumble on the slick parquet. Cursing all footwear that didn't have Vibram soles, she slowed her approach to join him with what she hoped was graceful nonchalance.

"You made it." Was that husky gush of sound her voice?

His once-over was a lingering caress. "You look great."

"This little old thing?" Had she remembered to clip off the price tag? Too late to look now. "I like your shoes."

"Not too understated?"

"Cute."

He grimaced. "They're my off-the-clock footgear so that people think I actually have time to do something recreational. Couldn't manage the laces, though." He had his hands tucked out of sight in the pocket of his jeans and, up close, she could see the pinch of discomfort at the corners of his eyes.

She reached for his arm. "Come on. I'll show you around and introduce you to my cousin."

The fabric of his jacket was as soft as his forearm was hard beneath it. *Don't cling. Don't clutch.* Her palms were sweaty as he let her squire him about, his attitude one of relaxed sophistication. He listened politely as she talked about each work and made pleasant conversation with those she knew. Idle banter came as naturally to him as profanity did to her, relieving her of that burden, so she could stand silently on his arm, watching him work the room. He chatted with the other guests, discussing artistic technique, the pros and cons of the ski slopes outside, and the use of art as an investment. He made it all seem effortless, his smile suavely charming, his low, gruff-edged voice as smooth as vintage Scotch, his conversation quick and intelligent and his looks…there was no faulting him there. Sleek, dark and flatteringly intense, yet aloof. And the pride of showing him off was foreign and exciting to her. He was the perfect party guest. Her guest.

Her *client,* warned a more familiar sensibility. Here, out of polite obligation. Because of the way her nerves were skittering, she needed to keep reminding herself of that. At the end of the evening, she had to let him go. Unconsciously, she hitched his arm in just a bit tighter. Then she slid a look up to explore the exquisite angles of his face the way those around them were studying the strong lines Karen used to depict one of the majestic mountain ranges. Beautiful, yet inaccessible and unyielding. And cold. A sigh whispered through her as she steered him toward her cousin.

"Karen, this is Xander Caufield. Alex, my cousin, the artist, Karen Parrish. All these wonderful paintings I can't afford are hers."

"Only because you won't let me give you one."

"Gifts don't pay bills."

Compared to Mel's bold, brassy appeal, Karen Parrish was a surprise. Pale, delicate, gracious—and in a wheelchair. A conservative beige knit dress covered her from neck to toe just as the sweep of her light strawberry-blond hair concealed part of her face. As she looked up at him, that fine hair slid back and revealed a webbing of scars on her cheek and neck. The remains of what had once been terrible burns. The hand she extended was slender, fragile, but her smile held a touch of the Parrish vinegar. She held his fingertips lightly as her thumb sketched over his bandaged knuckles. Because Mel had told her what the gauze concealed, her soft gray eyes clouded with tender sympathy.

"Mr. Caufield, a pleasure to meet any man who can come out looking better than my scrappy cousin after a fight."

His features relaxed into a wide, genuine smile that dazzled. "I had to work at it, Miss Parrish."

"It's Karen, and thank you for coming. I get nervous and Mel hates these things. It's nice to see a friendly face."

With a faint stirring of what she didn't want to believe was envy, Mel watched him respond to her pretty cousin with a warm charm she'd only had glimpses of before. And it only took Karen a brief squeeze of his fingertips.

"Your work is very good. I tend to collect acrylics and complex abstracts so I'm no expert." He shrugged. "Like I prefer jazz over this new age mood music you're playing.

Different but not better. I do like watercolors when they're well-done. They're…peaceful."

Karen scrutinized him. "You're not a very peaceful man, are you, Mr. Caufield?"

"Xander. And no, I don't have time for it."

She pressed his fingertips. "Make time and you'll have a better appreciation for the rest. Melody is just as bad. All this gorgeous serenity up here everywhere you look and you'd think she'd take two seconds to appreciate a sunset."

"I have a terrific appreciation for gorgeous things." It was difficult, but she managed not to slide a sidelong look at her escort. "If I didn't appreciate this plethora of natural wonders, I wouldn't be trying so hard to help keep them from burning down, now would I?"

Mel's wry remark unintentionally sobered her cousin. Her response was subdued. "Of course not."

Then, without explanation, Mel knelt to embrace her, hugging her with a husky whisper of "I'm sorry."

He was missing something. Something crucial to understanding the enigmatic creature at his side who'd stunned him stupid with her chameleon appearance. This wasn't the brassy pilot carelessly disinterested in her looks. The woman who'd greeted him at the door rivaled any of the blue blood debutantes who'd thrown themselves in his path at swanky events like this one since he was old enough to carry a credit card. Instead of being hotter than five-alarm chili, tonight she was a long, cool flame. Her hair was tamed back in a chic French braid. Her bold, bronzed features were enriched with hints of metallic beneath her brows, on her lips, dusted across her shoulders and glistening on the curve of her breasts. She wore no jewelry, nothing to outshine the sparkle in her dark eyes or to detract from the black dress that somehow was both elegant and mind-blowingly sexy at the same time. The inviting lines clung to her curves from the simple tank-styled top down to hug her waist and hips before ending in a teasing little flare at mid-thigh. And she wore heels, high, skinny and screaming fire-engine red. One look and he needed another shower.

The thing that set her apart from that long line of pedi-greed man-hunters he'd run through during his younger, wilder years was the fact that she was so endearingly uneasy with the fact that she was beautiful. That and the fact that she carried a gun and would kick his butt if he tried anything.

With her friends, she was loud, rude, one of the guys. With him, she was as cool and confident as the business end of the pistol she carried. But with Karen, when faced with her cousin's distress, she displayed a deep well of tenderness, the same sweet sympathy that had shocked him senseless in the hangar when she'd cared for his burns, had given him that thought-blanking kiss and had so briefly crumpled in his arms. What was he supposed to make of a woman like this, who changed her whole personality as quickly and casually as she changed her shoes? He wasn't sure and that made him more cautious than usual. Because she was beginning to intrigue him and he couldn't afford that.

Karen pushed her away, brushing off her concern with a smile. "Go find Charley. I sent him to see about some shipping costs and he hasn't made it back yet. I want to make sure he hasn't been distracted by the champagne. It's costing me a fortune and I'd just as soon save it for the guests." Intercepting her anxious glance, Karen added, "I'm sure your Mr. Caufield won't mind my company for a moment."

Xander's hand fit to Mel's elbow, supplying the leverage for her to gracefully regain her feet in her high heels. The gesture startled her. As if she needed his help to stand up. Like she'd needed his help with those thieves at the hotel. Or in rescuing one of her own from the flames. She took an uncertain step away from him, cautions quivering on the edge of objection. Because she didn't want to like depending on someone else quite so much.

He caught her look of alarm but had no chance to question it as she turned and hurried quickly toward the back of the gallery.

Seeing his brows lower in perplexity, Karen took pity on him.

"You unsettle her, which is a surprise because nothing much does."

He pulled his attention away from the rapidly retreating figure to regard the woman seated before him. "Why's that, do you think?"

"It doesn't matter what I think, Mr. Caufield. It's Mel who thinks you're so far out of her league you're orbiting a different planet."

"She'd be wrong, Miss Parrish."

His quiet answer satisfied her. She smiled at him. "This from a man lowering himself to the appreciation of watercolors."

She was mocking him gently and, slightly embarrassed by it, he glanced away from her knowing assessment only to find his interest captured by two paintings of Lake Tahoe, one a sunrise, one a sunset, both over the same fir-lined cove. The colors—the oranges melting into softer shades of gold and peach over sterling grays and blues fringed by spikes of forest-green—appealed to him because it stirred a sense of something he'd been missing…peace.

"I'd like those two paintings." He reached inside his coat.

She took a startled breath. "Don't you want to know how much they are?"

His smile took a cynical turn. "How can you put a price tag on serenity, Miss Parrish? Fill in the amount. My address is there on the check. Send the sunrise there."

"And the sunset?"

"Send that to your cousin."

She found him standing adrift in the tony crowd, staring up almost wistfully at a pair of landscapes while Karen was busy chatting up an elderly couple. For a moment, she kept her distance so she could look her fill without his notice. As if she could ever fill up completely with the sight of him. Stunning, complex, smart, brave beyond belief and hers, sort of, for the moment, a moment that was quickly passing. She had three more days, then he'd supply that bland little smile and be out of her life forever. There was nothing she could do about that. But how to make use of those three days toyed with her emotions, daring her, pushing her, tormenting her with possibilities—if she had the courage to act on the spark of attraction simmering between them; if she dared turn it up to a flame that could just as easily escape her control and burn her.

"What do you think?"

He glanced around at her question then returned to his study of the paintings. His expression was oddly quiet, unguarded, as he said, "She's very talented. Her work makes you yearn for…more."

"Yes, it does." And some of the sad, sweet longing teething upon her heart must have transferred to her tone, because he met her poignant gaze and didn't look away. The moment stretched out between them, deepening instead of growing uncomfortable. Until he asked, "Why do you do it?"

"Do what?"

"Take the chances that you do. Fly into that Satan's den just to spit in his eye. Why? I don't understand."

His question took her off guard, making her growl, "It's personal." Then, her initial defensiveness faded before a sudden insight, thinking of the thumbs-up he'd given as he'd stepped out the copter door. "Yes, you do. Because you're just like me. Why do you pretend to be that rigid unlikable snob when you're so much more?"

He reacted to her bluntness with a slow, glazing chill, stiffening his posture, icing his stare and freezing the angles of his face into harsh planes. And his answer was just as cold.

"It's personal."

"Sorry for the interruption." Karen's bright mood managed to chisel some of the frost from his stance, but even so, his smile was thin and reserved when he regarded her. Mel could feel her confusion, her glance skipping between them as she handed him a receipt. "There's a tracking number at the bottom."

"Did you buy something? Which one?"

Xander nodded toward the sunrise. "That one."

"Not the pair? It seems a shame to separate them."

"I don't have room and there's only so much *more* a man can handle." Then his testy mood eased as he enfolded Karen's hand in his. "I'll be expecting to hear great things, Miss Parrish."

"Thank you, Xander."

With a nod to Mel, he started away. She watched him go, paralyzed by indecision until her cousin nudged her with her chair.

"Go after him, Melody." Then she added something truly unbelievable. "He wants you to."

He'd almost made it to the door when he felt the light touch of her palm on the back of his arm. Just that slight brush of contact calmed his agitation. He stopped, took a steadying breath to get on top of all the dark emotions prowling through him then regarded the perplexing woman at his side.

"Thank you for inviting me. I enjoyed meeting your cousin. I like her." *I like you.*

"You're not fond of many people, are you?" Before his expression could shut down again, she gave a provoking grin. "I'm sorry. That's personal, too, I suppose."

He couldn't restrain a smile. "I've got to go."

Desperation goaded her into making a move. Her hand curled with a bit more possessiveness. "My feet are killing me and I'm dying of thirst. Do you have time to join me for a drink?"

He hesitated. She could see him weighing the situation with more consideration than her question warranted. At least on the surface. "All right. Where do you want to go?"

Her grin was pure hell.

"I know just the place."

Chapter 6

He could tell by the parking lot that she wasn't taking him to a place that served umbrella drinks. Dirty pickups and custom choppers lined up across the neon-lit front walk. Noting his surprise, she grinned as she cut off her engine.

"Don't tell me a preppie boy like you has never been to a strip club?"

His question was, why would she want to bring him to one?

Smoke and heavy metal pushed them back a step when the door opened. One sweeping glance told him it was not a tourist stop. Thankfully, there was no stage or pole to offer questionable entertainment. She'd been kidding about that. It was just a bar where burly working-class men tossed back shooters over mismatched tabletops. Tougher-looking waitresses wove between them in Daisy Dukes, sprayed-on Tshirts and enough makeup to plaster a wall. Leather-clad Harley boys crowded around the pool tables creating a colorful mural of tattoos. And every one of them regarded him and Mel with the same raised brows, wondering the same thing Xander was. What the hell were they doing there? It wasn't exactly the fashionable place to drop by after a gallery hop.

Then, Mel dragged him through the haze, oblivious to the stares she was garnering, around the corner of the bar, and there he got his answer.

Tables were pushed together for a group of about two dozen men already well into their third or fourth round, if the pyramid of empty pitchers was any indication. Spotting the two of them, they all rose to their feet to begin a loud chorus of catcalls and applause. It was then Xander recognized some of them from Mel's hospital bedside. These were the men she worked with. And in their midst was the youngster, Teddy Greenbaum, whom he'd pulled from the fire, looking no worse for wear. Still, Xander didn't quite get it until Greenbaum approached to snag him up for a fierce hug.

"You saved my bacon from crisping, man. I owe you big."

Grinning even wider, Mel stepped away to let her friends swarm the reluctant hero. Greenbaum shoved a shot and a beer at him and howled with approval as Xander tossed back the first and washed it down with the second. He moved rather stiff-legged as they pushed him to the tables, all demanding at once that he provide his rendition of the rescue. Surprised, overwhelmed by the attention, he let them shove him into a seat of honor. Then his gaze lifted to touch on hers. He smiled, a quick wide flash of white teeth. And just like that, her heart was gone.

She stood stunned for the longest minute as a strange sensation of warmth kept getting bigger and bigger within her chest, until she was sure her ribs would crack from the expanding pressure. She couldn't draw a full breath. Her vision blurred as her throat choked up around the wad of foreign emotion. She knew what it was. She'd felt it in varying degrees for her relatives, for the rowdy bunch gathered for the impromptu celebration. But never, ever, had the complex feelings stirred for anyone outside those select circles. She was too scared to call it by name. If she said it, if she thought it, she would have to own up to the fact that she was wildly, implausibly, head over heels for Xander Caufield.

She dropped into a chair at the far end of the line of tables, clutching her beer in panic. She watched him interact with her team, waiting for an awkwardness to arise that would single him out as not belonging. Waiting for him to withdraw behind the cold curtain of disdain he'd used to keep her at bay. He had nothing in common with this group who'd demanded the opportunity to thank him. But an amazing thing happened, the very last thing she'd expected. He fit in. Comfortably, completely, getting her friends to lean forward in anticipation of his tale, getting them to laugh at his claims of being thrust kicking and screaming into the role of savior. They knew it wasn't true. They'd heard of his reckless courage from Mel. They'd seen him all bloodstained and somber at her bedside. As he draped his arm companionably along the back of Teddy's chair and sucked the suds off his draft, suddenly Mel felt like the outsider with her strange, strong rifts of emotions.

No. She wouldn't allow it. She wouldn't care about her gorgeously groomed client, too afraid to open up her heart to that degree of hurt again. Those she entrusted, she tended to lose. The image of him boldly stepping out into air to disappear down into the smoke and flames below tormented her. The fright of it slapped the breath from her lungs, the strength from her knees. Someone that daring, that brave, with so little thought to his own safety was a risk she couldn't take.

But, while looking at him, hungering over him through her slitted stare, other feelings, deeper, darker, growled to life. She might not be able to care for him, but she did want him on a level that didn't have to go beyond surface sweat and heat. One that didn't require an investment to reap a reward. Remembering the taste of his mouth had her wetting her lips. And remembering the smoldering burn in his gaze as they rode the elevator told her all she needed to know. It might take a little push, but he wouldn't put up much of a fight against the attraction simmering between them. Not on an uninvolved, undemanding level. The only level she could allow.

Another round of beer splashed into their glasses. Another toast was lifted. Xander let the draft slide down all smooth and golden as he studied Mel Parrish over the rim of his mug. She was sprawled casually back in her chair, laughing over something one of the men had said to her. In the smoky setting, the sleek, classy front eased to become one of negligent sexiness. Every man at the table was aware of it, but they responded with good-natured indulgence, as if they were watching over a younger sister who was bent on raising hell.

And she was raising hell with him.

While he'd appreciated her styled beauty at the gallery, here, in an element more to her liking, she simply shone with a fierce earthy passion for life, for fun, for excitement. And danger. And oh, she was dangerous, sitting there with her shoulders rocking to the rollicking tune blasting from the jukebox, heedless of the way those at the bar followed the frisky jiggle of her breasts. Mel Parrish was starting fires she might not be able to extinguish. But he guessed that's what the table full of protective big brothers was for.

"Who's buying?"

The loud bellow brought a chorus of welcome from the men. And a tightness to Mel's features as Teddy hollered, "Hey, Quinn. Glad you could make it. Grab up a chair."

"Soon as I shake the hand of our guest of honor." A big hand thrust out to Xander. "Quinn Naylor. You must be Caufield 'cause you're the only one here who smells prettier than Mel."

Xander bared his teeth in a smile, scenting the hostility of the newcomer. Naylor was tall and lanky, a Texan from the sound of his accent. He had hawkish good looks and the natural arrogance of a leader. To a one, the men looked up to him. And Mel's dislike of him was a not-so-subtle undertow beneath the swell of goodwill. Xander surrendered his hand up to a crushing grip. He was aware of the other men grinning, waiting for him to wince, so he applied a little pressure of his own.

Surprise sparked in Naylor's eyes, followed by a shrewd reevaluation. He let go first and whooped, "Let's get this party started."

Shouts rose up along with glasses as Naylor turned the

chair opposite Xander and dropped into it. He folded his arms to lean on the back, his smile friendly, his steady gaze anything but.

"So you and Mel just swooped on in for a mission of mercy, did you?"

"And I'm damned glad they did." Teddy Greenbaum lifted his mug and gave his rescuer another sloppy hug about the neck.

Naylor's smile hardened. "Mel just let you, a civilian, jump right into the jaws of the beast, did she?"

"You shoulda seen him, Quinn. Last thing I remember was him zipping down that line without a suit on. Bravest damned thing you could imagine. I wouldn't have done it. And neither would you."

Naylor's eyes narrowed. "That's because we know better and we don't have that reckless hellcat pushing us out where we got no business going." His glance cut to a granite-faced Mel, then, having gotten the desired response, he was all charm and smiles again. "But that don't take nothing away from our hero here." He hoisted his glass and the others joined in. Xander drank more slowly, wondering what the other man was up to.

The jukebox began to pump out the pounding AC/DC standard "Back in Black." Naylor nodded his head in time to the aggressive beat then grinned at his friends.

"Seems to me nobody's given our friend here a proper thank-you." He pulled a twenty out of his jeans and waved it toward the end of the row of tables. "What do you say, Mel?"

Xander straightened in his seat, not sure what was being suggested, but the other firefighters took up the call of her name, urging, cajoling and whistling. Theirs was a cheerful provoking, but Naylor was all hard business. And seeing it, Mel rose slowly to meet his goading challenge. She came toward him, all angry, lethal sensuality and bent over to give him an unobstructed view down the front of her dress as she took his money and tucking it into her cleavage. He laughed, a mocking rather than amused sound and stood, boosting her up onto the tabletop. Slowly, her glare slashing into his, she shoved her fingers into her neatly braided hair and with a few determined pulls, shook it down into a fiery cascade. The seductive swing of her hips progressed into an undulation involving her whole body. The men in her audience produced twenties and began waving them, coaxing her down the length of the tables, stepping carefully around the empties, with a sinuous bump and grind to pluck them up. Because she shed nothing beyond her hairpins, and because the spirited mood was one of slightly naughty fun, not tawdry exploitation, Xander leaned back to enjoy her uninhibited dance. He and every other man in the bar.

When she had a handful of bills, Mel scooted off the tables, to the disappointment of the appreciative spectators, and went to stuff the money down Teddy Greenbaum's shirtfront. And as the youngster flushed to the roots of his hair, she bent to place a warm, wet kiss on his lips while the others hooted their approval. Then she straightened and turned her attention to a bemused Xander Caufield.

He gave a start as his chair was pulled away from the table and one of the older fellows sitting beside him leaned close to whisper, "Better sit on your hands, lest you be tempted to put them someplace they won't be welcomed."

He wondered over the warning until Mel's red high-heeled shoe was planted on the seat of his chair between the sprawl of his knees. His gaze flew up, detouring briefly to where the hem of her little black dress just barely managed to conceal all of Victoria's Secrets, then skimming up along the beckoning sway of her torso to meet the sultry gleam of her eyes. He wasn't sure it was a friendly stare. If she was trying to prove something to Naylor, he would just as soon be in a less vulnerable position. Then, still rocking to the beat of the music, she leaned close, her arms circling his neck. Her hard veneer crumbled to one of pure tease, prompting his response.

"I'm reaching for my wallet."

And she laughed, remembering those mildly spoken words and their explosive aftermath.

The song changed to the boisterously raunchy "You Shook Me All Night Long." Mel stepped back and before Xander could release his breath in a shaky rattle, she'd snagged his lapels, tugging him toward the dance floor.

Once on the flashing disco-era lit squares, Mel fit her palms to his back pockets and sank into a hip-grinding shimmy that placed her taunting features at his zipper level. Enough was enough. He caught one of her hands, jerked her up so they were eye to suddenly combative eye, then sent her spinning out under the bridge of his arm, reeling her back in with a snap that knocked her flush against his chest. While she grabbed for her breath, he grinned down at her, his look so filled with the promise of sinful excitement, it lit her enthusiasm like a backfire in the brush. Curling his arm about her waist, he walked her back through a series of fast steps then let her drop in a dip that had her hair brushing the floor before hauling her up into his arms.

And then she smiled back, releasing a breathy little laugh that dropped right to his loins.

"What's a nice little jazz and latte conservative like you know about dancing to music like this?" she taunted.

"I wasn't always a nice little jazz and latte conservative. I was…more."

And to prove it, his palms clasped her waist, tugging her into him, letting her ride the bold rock and roll of his hips to the provoking beat of the song.

"And what about you? That wasn't exactly a folk dance you were doing."

"It's the crew's favorite fund-raiser. I've never been able to figure out why."

"Oh, I have a good idea."

She revolved to lean back against him, conforming to the rhythmic sway of his knees and pulse of his thighs. He started getting all sorts of ideas as he pressed her closer, one hand on her undulating belly while the other snaked her arm about his neck. She felt his grin as he gave her a taste of what else he had been before becoming the uptight über controlled Xander.

Fun, she decided. He'd been fun. Someone who climbed rocks and base jumped. Someone who could dance as if they were having wild, unbridled, fully clothed sex standing up in a room full of people and not care. A daredevil. Like her.

Exhilarating.

Dangerous.

The song ended. She stepped quickly out of his embrace and broke from the gaze that was as lustily hot as their moves had been. She wanted more of what those moves suggested, on a horizontal plane, and was scared right down to the reinforced toes of her panty hose that once wasn't going to be enough.

As if her emotions weren't spinning through a tidal pull of desire, she turned to a surprised then blushing Teddy Greenbaum and beckoned him with the waggle of her fingers to join her on the dance floor. Leaving Xander to return to his seat knotted tight with frustration.

"She's playing with you, son," Quinn confided as he slopped more beer into his glass. And the smugly sympathetic way he said it struck like a kidney punch.

"Voice of experience?" he growled.

Naylor's grin was goading. "Oh, yeah."

Xander took a long drink and considered crunching through the edge of the mug just to have something lethal to spit back at the Texan who'd been Mel Parrish's lover. And because he didn't want to admit that the sudden blackness of his mood was due to Naylor's enviable state, Xander watched her dancing with the young firefighter through hard, dispassionate eyes. His snub chafed Quinn Naylor, who wasn't used to being ignored.

"Mel tells me you're a real tough guy."

Xander pretended not to hear him. He'd wasted enough of his misspent youth in smoky bars to know where things were heading if he didn't do something to defuse the situation. Naylor was deliberately provoking him into doing something stupid so he'd have the chance to beat the crap out of him. He could feel the remembered cut of his braces filling his mouth with blood. But instead of coming up with something innocuous or amusing that would calm Naylor's belligerence, he took another drink and regarded the firefighter with a heavy-lidded chill.

"Don't get in my face."

It was about Mel and they both knew it.

Naylor laughed. "Well, son, that's not my intention at all. Just looking to have a good time."

At Xander's expense. Yeah, he got that. And his jaw clenched as he followed Greenbaum leading Mel through an awkward two-step to some countrified rock song. She was flushed and laughing and the vise squeezing his insides twisted a notch tighter.

Xander turned to Quinn to ask politely, "Are you this big a jerk with everyone or just the ones Mel's interested in?"

All traces of humor fell from the Texan's expression. "You got an attitude and a big mouth, boy, and I don't much like either of them."

"And how would you suggest we resolve that problem?"

"What are you up to, Quinn?" Mel demanded as she rejoined the table. She could sense the anticipating tension in her friends and that was never a good sign.

"You are so suspicious. Just a little man-to-man talk with your pretty friend here. He was about to prove just how tough he is with a little good-natured competition." And Naylor swept the table clean between them.

Obviously everyone but Xander knew what was coming because quick bets were being made in low, excited voices.

"You ready to serve it up, boy?"

"Quinn, stop it," Mel hissed.

"What's on the menu, good buddy?"

Mel gripped Xander's shoulder. "Don't get into this with him. Time to go."

"Better listen to her, pretty boy."

"Shut up, Quinn."

"Why you mad at me, darlin'? Seems like he's the one with something to prove. Like going down into that fire thinking his sheer arrogance would protect him." Naylor's eyes glittered.

"Alex, don't be a fool."

He hadn't been a fool for a long time and he was thinking he was due. "What's on your mind, Ace? Bare knuckles or Mensa questions?"

That made Quinn pause, but only for a moment. He dropped his elbow in the center of the table and put up his hand with a low growl, "You want to take me down so bad, here's your chance. Or are you afraid you'll break a nail?"

"Alex."

But Xander was shedding his coat. The black T-shirt he wore beneath it was sleeveless, displaying impressively cut arms and a surprising tribal armband tattoo ringing his left bicep. "It's just for fun, Mel. Hold this for a minute." He passed her his jacket then notched his elbow in next to Naylor's. And he put up his hand, bandages and all, letting Quinn take it in a crushing grip. Sweat popped on his brow the way veins did along his inner arm, but there was no change in his impassive expression or flicker in the flat black of his stare. He could see Quinn's surprise at his resistance, a surprise that focused into an angry determination in front of all his peers.

When he didn't get the quick victory he expected—or any momentum in their stalemated give and take—Naylor lashed out under table with the toe of his steel-plated boots, trying to break Xander's concentration. When Xander refused to slacken his effort as the onlookers shouted encouragement, another, harder kick made his unexpectedly tenacious opponent wince. And that's when Xander decided all was fair.

Without lifting his elbow off the table, he lunged forward, butting his antagonist full in the face. Naylor howled but only intensified his grip. So Xander came back at him, using the side of his head to deliver a solid blow to Naylor's temple. And then he drove the Texan's wrist to the table with a satisfying thump.

There was a long silence. Xander tensed, blood hot, ready to take it outside, because there was no way he was backing down. Then Greenbaum slapped him on the back with a cheery "Pay up, fellas. Told you he was good for it."

Naylor's glare skewered Xander from across the table-top. Agony pounded up from his fingertips and gathered to hammer inside his head. He blinked, his eyes beginning to cross and roll when Mel leaned over to slap the back of his aching head, then reached over to do the same to Xander.

"Stupid boys. There's too much testosterone at this table." She grabbed up one of the chuckling firefighters and hauled him toward the dance floor. Xander and Quinn stared after her.

When Xander's wandering hand couldn't seem to find his beer, Quinn pushed it into his path begrudgingly, "You are a tough little SOB, aren't you?"

"I don't know how to step back when I can push forward."

Quinn laughed, nodding at that philosophy. He gripped Xander's elbow. "C'mon. Looks like you need something stronger."

As he stumbled out of the chair, Xander began to think what he needed was the hospital. Splayed along the bar top, he winced from the towel Naylor pressed to his brow. It came away red. Quinn chuckled at his expression.

"Son, I've been stupid all my life, but you don't have the look of someone prone to it."

"Not for a long, long time. Kind of surprised myself. I'd forgotten how much pride hurts." He swapped the towel for the chilling compress of Jack on ice in a glass.

"She'll do that to a man."

He was talking about Mel, and Xander wasn't sure he wanted to go there with this man who knew her intimately. But he couldn't pass up on the chance to learn more. Then Naylor stunned him with an earnest demand.

"You be careful with her. She's not as tough as you are. Or as tough as she'd like us to think. Just thought I'd let you know that, seeing's how you'll be the one going home with her tonight."

Chapter 7

Naylor's blunt assumption focused the massive ache from Xander's head to a much lower region.

"Don't pack a bag. We don't call her One Night for nothing."

Xander's gaze drifted to the dance floor. "Why's that?"

"Because that's all she'll invest in any man. There's never a second time around. Not even for me."

Xander frowned and Quinn laughed at the look.

"I'm not saying she makes a weekly or even a monthly habit of it. Hell, I don't even remember the last time she left here with some poor fool on her arm. She likes to play, sure, but not for keeps. Just so you know. She's got other demons on her mind and until she gets on top of them, she's not much good for any long haul, not in the sky, not on the sheets."

But that wasn't telling him nearly enough. "Why?"

Quinn turned to rest his elbows on the bar, sipping his drink as he watched a free-spirited Mel dance. He was in love with her, Xander realized, but it was the hard, bitter kind of emotion that came from knowing it wasn't returned. "She got burned by the beast when she was a kid. Lost her mom in the same fire that crippled her cousin Karen. She wasn't able to get to them through the flames. Then her daddy, Patrick, he was a daredevil, that one, he went down in a firestorm trying a rescue stunt he had no business thinking he could pull off. She pushes so hard because she's afraid of it, of the fire. It's the fear that makes her too reckless to rely on. A man can't trust someone with that much raw nerve. That's why I pulled her off the crews. And that's why, at the moment, she hates my guts."

It's personal, she'd told him and now he knew why.

The music shifted to Aerosmith's sultry "Sweet Emotion." As Mel was returning to the table, breathless and moist with perspiration, Xander stepped into her path and tried to lead her back toward those winking panels.

She set her heels, glaring at him in challenge. "Done showing off?"

His grin broke wide with unrepentant mischief. "Maybe."

Then his arm scooped about her waist and, with her hand trapped in his, he whirled her about until she was pressed close, matching him step for step, her heart beat for beat. She swayed against him, her head tucked into his shoulder, her palm rubbing slowly over the swell of his tattooed upper arm. And as the music quickened with a harder, faster pulse, they continued to move together in a sensuous side-to-side, to a rhythm far removed from a noisy barroom before a drunken audience of her peers.

With her eyes shut, he filled up her senses. With the compelling textures of his body from hot, slick skin and the broad rock wall of his chest to the possessive curl of his arm about her waist. With the remembered scent of his designer cologne chafing against that of beer and whiskey. With the way he made her feel surrounded, protected, special, overwhelming her, making her go all weak but contrarily feel stronger.

Go after him, Mel. He wants you to.

She couldn't let this moment pass. She couldn't let this man go untested, untried, or she would never forgive herself. Never mind that he was leaving, never mind that the closer she let him get, the harder the inevitable parting was going to hit her. If she let her guard down all the way, she feared the pain of loss would be nearly fatal. Her palm moved restlessly along his bare arm and her other hand slipped from his to cup the back of his dark head. This was close, this was nice and safe. She nuzzled against the side of his neck. His arms tightened, folding her in closer still. Her mouth moved upon the hot column of his throat, tasting the hurried beat of matching desire as it built there, and below, where he pressed her into the cove of his thighs. That exquisite sense of want sharpened as his lips stirred warm upon her brow. Without a thought to consequence, she lifted her face to let him capture her with his kiss.

Pleasure, sweet and aching, woke beneath that deep, seducing kiss. The smooth, firm mastery of his mouth moving over hers didn't take or demand but gave with an unpressuring thoroughness that had her shaking to her soul. Oh, how he wrung the heart from her with the simple elegance of motion, sliding, sweeping, coaxing her to moan his name in a delightfully dazed confusion.

They'd stopped moving, unaware of other couples spinning around them. Lost to the luxury of his lips, she heard herself whisper his name. Heard the soft, yearning tone of a woman vulnerable and inviting…what, exactly? For him to take more than she could ever share? For him to take advantage of her loss of control and wound her beyond repair? No. Not even for him.

She took a saving breath, flushing romantic notions from heart and mind, concentrating instead on the basic pulse of uncomplicated need. She wouldn't think of him as Alex. That was far too dangerous. She would think of him as a lusty bounce on starched sheets, as Xander Caufield of the chiseled, emotionless features who would have great sex with her, but not make love. And afterward, she'd be able to walk away unscarred.

She surged up against him, beginning an aggressive assault on his mouth. Devouring, plunging, sucking up his senses. She could feel his start of surprise, but he didn't pull away. She bumped and ground into him to the beat of the next song, rubbing along his hard angles, taking his hands and placing them at the backs of her thighs, letting the strength of her desire carry them both recklessly away. Wanting, needing the dark swells of passion to purge her of tender ideas born at the first amazing foray of his lips. This was safer. Primal, clear-cut, and honest. Damn, it was honest, the fierce, hot way they desired each other. And she pursued him with a vengeance.

He wasn't sure what sparked the change in her. One instant she was nearly liquid in his arms, responding with a surprising malleability to his touch. Then, the heat turned up like an acetylene torch, scorching him on the outside the way her receptiveness had thawed his inner chill. Her mouth was voracious, hungry. Her hands prowled over him, impatient, bold, yanking his T-shirt from the waistband of his jeans so her palms could push underneath to drag over his flat middle. The notion that she might shuck him right down to the skin in the middle of the dance floor never progressed beyond an anxious murmur, not when up against the roar in his blood that didn't care if she did. As long as she didn't stop. She led, he followed, as the quick steps of their dance cut across the now-crowded floor and into smoky shadow. Without leaving his lips, she dragged him into the service area near the kitchen and pushed him back through a door marked, Private. Employees Only.

The pungent scent of cleanser and hand soap told him they were in a washroom. It was dark, the sounds from the bar a muted whisper beneath the rough frenzy of their breathing. He heard Mel snap the latch on the door but as he groped for a light switch, she panted, "Leave it off." What they wanted, what they needed from each other, was more suited to darkness.

She shoved him back against a small sink, kissing him hard, the violence of it alarming, exciting. His hands were in the tangle of her hair, twisting, trying to control her frantic assault on his mouth, his throat, as she worked the fastening of his pants. Then she was dropping down and his hands flew backward, grabbing at the sink for balance. His world careened wildly at the sudden hot swirl of her mouth over the length of him. His mind went blank as a flood of hot sensation pulled him under, dunking him in black, turbulent waters before he had a chance to catch his breath. Then she was lifting off him, her movements hurried as she stepped out of her shoes, shimmied out of her stockings. Within a heartbeat, she was fixed back on his mouth, situating his hands on her bared hips. Clamping his face between the press of her palms, she devoured his senses along with any threads of resistance he had left.

Roughly, he turned them both, hoisting her up onto the edge of the cold sink basin as she snared him in an urgent, compelling twist of arms and legs.

And then he was inside her, buried deep, sheathed in fire.

He drew a marveling breath.

When he would pause to savor the sensations of having her hot and tight around him, she pushed past the acquainting phase with a brusque impatience, beginning a hard, driving motion with her hips, with her mouth. When he tried to slow her down, to set a pace they could enjoy together, she wouldn't let him. She fought against his attempt to bring intimacy into their hurried mating. She spoke his name in harsh syllables along with the explicit act she demanded from him.

Xander. She called him Xander.

And he stopped, his thoughts taking precedence over their runaway passions. Because there was nothing passionate in what she was doing. What she wanted was sex, plain and simple, down and dirty. And there was nothing the least bit simple about what he wanted from her.

"Mel, stop. We're not prepared for this."

She didn't want to listen. Her fingertips spread wide across the angles of his face, her mouth seeking his, seeking to suck him back into that uncontrollable tidal pool. But he was unwinding her legs from their clasp about his waist, was le-

vering back, pulling away and out to leave her emptied and
dazed.

"What's wrong?" she gasped in confused frustration.

He couldn't think of a way to explain it. He didn't understand it himself so he said with a whisper of regret, "I have to go. I'm sorry. I shouldn't have let you start something I couldn't finish."

She went still. Her breathing rasped, loud and raw in the darkness, becoming a low, wounded growl.

"You bastard."

She shoved him back, scrambled off the sink, her angry pants for breath tearing on the sound of sobs as she wriggled into her underwear. A brief flash of light from the hallway blinded him as she fled the room.

Slowly, he straightened his clothing then braved the overhead lights so he could splash water on his face. When he looked in the mirror, he saw a bastard. And when he glanced down, he saw Mel's abandoned red heels. Picking them up, he forced himself to return to the bar area.

She was on the dance floor in the beefy arms of one of the bikers. As she provoked her partner with the inviting sway of her hips, she skewered Xander with a look that was coldly eviscerating before pouring her attentions back upon her burly companion. Grimly, he returned to the table of firefighters, most of whom were too adept at reading the significance of her shoes in his hand and her hips grinding into someone else's to say anything or were just too drunk to care.

Quinn took the red shoes from him. "Son," he drawled out. "You have the look of stupid all over you again."

Xander could only nod as he collected his coat. When

his focus was drawn back to the dance floor, Quinn's tone softened.

"We'll see she gets home safe."

And just like that, Xander was shut out of their inner circle where briefly he'd felt like he belonged.

And when the next door opened to him after a short drive to the lake's west side and his oldest friend gave him a quick once-over to demand, "What the hell are you doing to yourself?" all he could say was, bleakly, "I don't know anymore."

He sat on the ledge of the side porch, his soul as empty as the big resort hotel behind him. The workmen and skeleton-crew staff had gone home hours ago and quiet settled in around him with a lonesome sigh. Hugging tented knees, he eyed the distant ridge where a faint red glow highlighted the tree line. Even with so much distance between the resort and the blaze, the stench of smoke curled on the night breeze.

The investigative reports he'd been waiting for rested on the broad stone stab beside him. One read through told him everything he needed to know and the truth had him aching worse than the pain gnawing at his nerve endings.

He didn't know what he was doing. Somewhere along the line, Mel Parrish had managed to do the impossible. She had begun to matter.

"Here you go. This should have you in a fetal position in about a half hour. I take them for my back when I don't need to function on a level above baked squash for at least eight hours. You look due for some serious time in a vegetative state."

"Thanks, Kyle." As his friend frowned at his subdued

tone, he took the pill and swallowed it, hoping oblivion would come soon. He could feel his friend's concern, but didn't have the strength to address it. Not tonight.

"Anything in there you can use?"

Xander followed his gesture to the stack of information. He answered in a quiet monotone. "Everything I expected."

Everything he'd begun to hope he wouldn't find out. Debts, huge and consuming then suddenly paid in full. And he knew with a damning certainty that when he checked the payment dates, they'd coincide with the suspicious fires.

He heard the creak of wicker as Kyle D'Angelo settled into one of the chairs arranged along the porch. He could feel the questions he hadn't yet asked. Vaguely, Xander wondered what to tell him. The truth? Wouldn't that shock him beyond all reason? That he'd taken on a group of knife-wielding thugs over an empty courier case? That he'd dropped from a helicopter into a forest fire to impress a woman? And that the woman he was investigating had him so dazed and bedazzled that less than an hour ago he'd been rutting in the throes of unprotected sex in an employee bathroom? And that the only reason he'd walked—no ran—away was because he hadn't wanted the one night they might share together to be mindlessly hot and heavy in the restroom of a bar. He took a long, deep drag of air and expelled it slowly as softly blurred edges began to gather around his thoughts.

"Colorado's not that far," Kyle was saying. "Think about it. Cigars, tub, booze, no worries."

Xander didn't respond. He blinked against the prisms of light haloing his vision as the intense agony of his mood quieted to a soreness of spirit. Kyle continued on as if indifferent to his pain, but he knew that was far from the case. If there was anything Kyle understood, it was misery.

"Just a quick flight. We'd be there by dawn. We could have your hot little pilot shuttle us up and—" The words stopped so abruptly, Xander slid a reluctant glance his way. Kyle was staring at him, seeing far too much in the tragic set of his features. "No." A firm objection. "No, no, no, no, no."

Hearing the censure in his friend's disbelieving tone, Xander let his head sag down between his knees, crossing his arms over the top of it as if he could protect himself from the whiplash to come as he murmured miserably, "Angie, what am I going to do? I think I'm in—"

"Stop! Don't you ever say it out loud. You know better. We both do. Xander, look at me." When he wouldn't, Kyle sighed heavily. "Aw, hell. I knew it. You don't want to go there. I've been there and it's a bad, bad place. A place for suckers and fools. and we're not either of those things, are we? Xander?"

"Tonight I am."

Cursing, Kyle got up and crossed to the low wall, pacing for a minute before taking a seat next to his friend. He regarded him almost angrily for another long minute then, with an irritated sigh, eased his hand across the slumped shoulders.

"She called me Xander."

"So? That's your name."

"It wasn't always."

A terrible sense of dread began building in Kyle D'Angelo. "We go back a long way, bro. I remember who you were before. You don't want to go back there to being that guy."

"I made her cry."

The low, punishing way he said that made Kyle curse again. "So? She's the job, Xander. The job you had me go out on a limb for with my sister, to pull the strings you needed. When Tess finds out I played her to get your pilot in with her husband's group, that nice little pregnant lady is going to show up on my front steps with that big gun she carries and shoot me dead. If you want to feel sorry for somebody, feel sorry for me."

"I'm sorry."

The quiet whisper of regret wasn't what D'Angelo wanted to hear and Xander knew it. The meds were pulling him down the rabbit hole. His hands were numb and all the sharp angles of hurt around his heart and mind were starting to melt away along with his bones. Placing his friend into the difficult spot of slapping some sense into him.

"Don't get torn up over this. Didn't you learn anything putting me back together piece by piece? What did you tell me to do? Screw her if you have to before she screws you over."

"I'm such an ass. Why do you listen to me?"

"Because you were right. And you listen to me right now. Pull up before you hit the ground. Xander…Alex, she's not going to want you once she finds out who you are any way. Don't do this to yourself."

"She doesn't want me now. Not…me. What's wrong with who I am that it's never enough? What's wrong with me?"

"You're drunk and you're flying about two feet out of body on my Vicodin. Things will look better in the morning."

"I'm not really a scary guy."

Another soft curse then a mutter of, "Well, you're scaring the hell out of me. And I'm sorry."

Sorry? Xander didn't understand.

"Alex, I talked to your dad the other day."

The words took him like a fist to the ribs. He sucked a quick breath and started to rear back in alarm, but Kyle's hand fisted in his jacket, holding him in place as he cried out in anguish, "Why? Why would you do that?"

"Because you won't."

He tried to say more, to express anger or objection but it was too late to get over the huge knot of shocked emotion wedged up under his Adam's apple. He made an incoherent sound that Kyle misinterpreted, perhaps intentionally, as a request to hear more.

"He said he was doing okay. That you weren't supposed to worry. But he is worried about you."

Strangling on his conscience, Xander shook his head.

"He wants to see you, Alex."

"No."

"He wants to talk to you."

"No."

Kyle's grip tightened across the shake of his friend's shoulders. "He wanted me to tell you that he forgives you."

"No." With that tortured cry, Xander lunged backward, trying to shove off the sympathetic hand, trying to wriggle out of his jacket, out from under his guilt. Unable to escape either, he finally hugged his knees, barricading himself behind them.

"He wanted to tell you that himself. Alex, talk to him. I'll take you anytime you're ready to go."

"No. I can't go. You know why. You know w̶

"I do know, but I still think you're wrong. Wrong ̶
wrong now. And staying away isn't helping. It's been
years. Years. Isn't it time for you to give the both of you a
break?"

"Not until I make it right. Not until I've got someone
else to put in that cell instead of him." He took a deep, fractured breath and lifted his head. His eyes were glazed with
sorrow, with the effects of the drug, but an unsteady pass
of his hand across them brought back the sharpness and
focus. "And I'm close, Kyle. I'm so close." He picked up
the papers, the bitter trail that led to the Parrishs' door. His
hands clenched, crumpling the sheets into a wad before
flinging them down to the porch floor.

"Alex, maybe you need to take a step back and let
someone else handle it. Let me take care of it for you. You
know I will."

There was the out he'd been searching for, the chance
to remove himself from the misery of conflict ever tightening within his chest. The means to let go with some scrap
of honor. And it was tempting. As tempting as the cigars,
the tub, the booze…and the woman. But not tempting
enough.

"It has to be me. It's important for him to know that."

And he rolled away from the wall onto hands and
knees to gather up the scattered pages with their incrimi-
nating truths.

And one of those truths was that he wasn't Alex Caufield anymore.

Chapter 8

The sound of engine tinkering drew a groggy Mel into the hangar bay squinting like a mole against the daylight. Charley's feet projected out from under the nose of the Ranger, but the real breath-sapping surprise was the denim-clad backside of Xander Caufield confronting her from out of the engine cavity. For a moment, she just stared, appreciatively following the snug contours the way her palms had the night before.

The night before…

Her hands rose to her temples, trying to press that searing event from her head. Had she really dragged her client into a dark washroom with the purpose of seduction?

And he'd refused her.

She had a scant second to adjust her expression as he straightened and looked her way. Alexander Caufield III with grease smudged on his brow was her every unfulfilled fantasy come to life.

"'Morning." His was a nice, neutral greeting.

"This is the last place I ever expected to see you." Let him take that however he wanted.

She couldn't tell how her words were received. He allowed a bland smile and the moment stretched out awkwardly between them. She usually wasn't forced to deal with her mistakes so soon after making them. It didn't help that her traitorous body came tinglingly alive with the remembered feel of him—his taste, his scent, his size and shape so briefly claiming a place within her. In her weakened state, if he'd shown any sign of welcome, she would have stepped over Charley on her way to his lips without the interference of a single objecting brain cell.

But there was no invitation in his steady dark eyes. And she stuffed in her emotional shirttails in a frantic attempt to look composed and unaffected by that deliberate rebuff.

"Mellie, grab me a box head," Charley hollered. "Xander brought over breakfast and was good enough to offer a hand when I couldn't get your lazy butt out of bed."

His reference to bed brought home her appearance. She was wearing a well-washed Metallica T-shirt that stopped just shy of her shocking-pink string bikini underwear. And on her bare feet, she wore her cozy multicolor fuzzy slippers. It had seemed like a fuzzy-slipper morning when she'd crawled from bed. Now she wished for those red high heels as Xander's gaze sketched briefly down her legs to rest on the silly blobs of fluff. That got a twitch of reaction that was quickly repressed. He was probably laughing at her ridiculousness. Vowing not to care, she scuffled over to the tool chest to select the wrench, wondering if she should just drop it through the hole onto her uncle's head. What was he thinking, asking for Xander's help?

And what was he doing here, anyway?

She glanced at the box of doughnuts on the compressor next to two mugs of coffee. The implied intimacy with her family blew up her temper like a quick blast from that coiled hose.

"I would have figured you for a fresh-squeezed and blintz kind of guy."

"Grab that for me, Xander."

His attention called away by the request, she couldn't see his expression when he said, "My appetites are fairly basic in the morning. And if I want something squeezed, I do it myself."

She tensed, remembering the grip of his hands on the cheeks of her rump. Her tone was sharp. "What are you doing here? I don't have anything scheduled for you until tomorrow."

He came up out of the engine space to lean on his forearms. He was wearing a dark green T-shirt that did amazing things to his eyes. Eyes that regarded her unblinkingly. "Just waiting for the guys to pick me up. Charley needed someone without any real skill to lift while he tightened."

And she tightened, recalling the strength in those very skilled hands where he had lifted her atop the sink. "Guys? What guys?"

"Quinn and Teddy."

Her guys. An unfamiliar growl of territorial invasion

rumbled. "What do they want with you?" *And why am I just now hearing about this?*

"They offered to take me up with them this morning while they scope out the fire."

"It's not exactly spectator entertainment," she snapped. "I thought you'd seen quite enough of the fire for one lifetime."

"I don't find it entertaining," he drily retorted. "It's interesting."

"Interesting?" Her mood clenched like a fist. "What I find interesting is your trivializing matters of life and death."

"Really? I thought that was the one thing we had in common."

"Xander, up a little."

He looked down to make the adjustments, giving Mel a chance to suck a breath through gritted teeth. And then he knocked the wind from her. "Do you want to go?"

"Go?"

"Up with us. You might want to change out of those slippers, though." He glanced at her and the glint of amusement in his eyes melted away her anger with an annoying ease.

"I'll grab a quick shower."

And there it was. The hot flare of want behind his primly smoldering front. She hadn't imagined it the night before.

So, if he wanted her so much, why the skittery hesitation? Something to do with whomever he was meeting after her abrupt dismount? Had he gone right from her kisses to someone else?

Wishing she'd hit him with the bathroom sink, she scowled and shuffled back to her rooms, where she made record time hurrying herself back together.

* * *

When she'd gone, Xander felt safe enough to release his suspended breath. Those slippers. Just when he'd thought he had her carefully, cautiously relegated out of the path of his emotions, something as sappy and silly as fuzzy footwear neatly ripped through his practiced reserve. He wouldn't again make the mistake of thinking he had any immunity whatsoever where Mel Parrish was concerned. He'd have to keep her at arm's length as much as possible and step up his investigation. Because every minute he failed to resist Mel was a minute of freedom he was denying his father.

A saving sense of purpose returned, erasing the softer lines from his face.

"A little more to the left. That's got her." Charley pushed out from under the Ranger, wiping his hands on a shop rag. "Should keep the pieces together a little longer. Seems like that's all we do these days."

"What's that?"

"Take shortcuts."

"Tough times?"

"When aren't they?"

This was the opening Xander had been looking for. He eased up to it carefully as he backed down the step stool to the concrete floor. "Probably doesn't help being grounded during the fire season."

A heavy sigh. "Not when you depend on every penny just to get by. But then you don't have those kind of troubles, do you?"

Because there was no edge to his question, Xander answered honestly. "No. Money's never been one of my problems."

"Lucky you. It's eating Mel up alive, but she's got too much of her daddy's pride to go begging for gypsy jobs from other crews. Quinn needs her as much as she needs him, but neither one of them will budge an inch." He slid a speculative look up to where Xander was leaning back against the bird. "Was kind of surprised to see him bring her home last night. Maybe they're patching things up."

Holding a steady expression made the muscles of his face hurt. "Are they close, Mel and Quinn?"

"Like oil and vinegar. He got his start with Mel's daddy. Good pilot. Good man. Rubs Mel the wrong way having to go to him for work now. Things used to be a lot different when Patrick was alive. She's so much like him. Hell on wheels."

"How long ago did he die?"

"Going on seven years. Went down in a blaze of glory, just the way he wanted. Left us with this. And a stack of bills we're still trying to dig out from under. Paddy never met a woman or a game of chance he could walk away from. And never had a lick of luck with either one. If it wasn't for Mel's business sense we'd have gone under a long time ago. She's a sharp one, Mel. Always coming up with a job, always finding a way to make ends meet. There's nothing she wouldn't do to keep this company in the air."

Nothing.

"'Course, I'm not much help to her. I'm a good grease monkey but if I could still fly, we'd be back on our feet in no time."

"Why can't you? If you don't mind me asking."

"Scar tissue in my lungs. Doesn't mix with altitude. FAA pulled my ticket."

"Fire?"

"The same bitch that took Mel's mom and nearly Karen. Going on fifteen years now. None of us were ever the same after that." His voice still held a note of sorrow and his eyes a heavy weight of something Xander recognized all too easily. Guilt.

"Is that what put your daughter in a wheelchair?"

He nodded, his eyes welling up. "My little girl. Broken, burned and scarred and not a damned thing I can do."

"There's no surgery?"

"Went through years of it just to get her where she is now. With no insurance. The bills were unbelievable. She finally said no more to the pain and the cost and made peace with it. She's the lucky one. She recovered better than the rest of us."

"And Mel? Was she injured, too?"

"Not where it shows."

Xander shut off the part of him that would care what he'd meant by that. He didn't want to imagine the kind of scars such a thing would leave on a little girl. And he didn't want to remember the way she'd clung to him here in the hangar after pulling him up from the consuming jaws of the fire. Her fragile, painful past was not his concern. Unless it related to his goal.

"She had to grow up so fast that summer, to take care of all of us. Twelve years old and already learning how to help her daddy stretch a dime into a dollar."

And how had they done that? Xander wondered, using a harsh cynicism to crush the sympathy he felt for these people and all they'd endured. Had they found a way to strike back at the flames by turning arson into the family business? Was the awful guilt he saw swimming in Charley's eyes from knowing he started the fire that destroyed his family? Or had Patrick Parrish's reckless lifestyle forced him to resort to illegal means to raise his daughter alone? Or, more sobering, had Mel inherited more than his carelessness? Had she discovered a coldly calculating way to help those she loved survive? He didn't like any of those scenarios, but he couldn't ignore them. Because he'd seen the evidence and he knew huge debt didn't just disappear on its own.

And because the only way his own debt would be paid was to place the blame on one of them. Or all of them.

Those things were working through his mind, teething on his conscience when Mel returned. Before he was aware of her standing there watching him, too much of that turmoil played out across his expression. When he glanced up, she wasn't quick enough to cover her alarm. Because she had something to hide? He couldn't exactly ask her. So he arranged his features into a neutral mask. And he could see her caution, her wariness as she approached.

"Don't let me interrupt," she drawled. "But be warned, Charley. If you're trying to solicit a little sympathy from Mr. Caufield, you'll be sorely disappointed. He doesn't have time for that type of thing, do you, Xander?"

He met her fierce glare with an unblinking cool. "No. Not really."

And Charley, who was used to his niece's brusque bad behavior, was embarrassed enough to mutter, "Mel, there's no call for you to be so rude to a guest."

"He's not a guest. He's all business. Isn't that right?"

"That's right."

As she watched her harsh words back him up behind that cold arrogant wall, Mel felt ashamed and almost at once began to mourn the loss of the companionable ease of moments before. But an approachable, relaxed Xander Caufield presented too much of a threat to her own wobbly composure. Because of what had happened at the bar. Or rather, because of what hadn't. He was safer when on the defensive, when the barriers were up between them. And as unsatisfactory as that was, it was preferable to the tense vulnerability he stirred within her. Because he'd walked away and she couldn't seem to let that go. She wanted him, wanted to finish what they'd started, and at the same time, was so afraid of getting tangled up in those emotions, her heart was racing like a locomotive engine pulling a load uphill.

But Charley was right. She didn't have to be so rude.

Xander's stance grew taut by increasing degrees as she approached. She couldn't miss it. By the time she stood before him, he was pulled tighter than kite silk on a 100-pound test line. She caught him by the fingertips so she could examine the crude wrapping about his palm.

"How are your hands?"

He truly couldn't answer. All he could feel was her gentle touch. "Fine," he managed.

She frowned, calling him on that bluff. Sympathy welled up in her eyes. She couldn't suppress it so she tried to distract herself from it by lightly brushing the split skin on his brow where two frustratingly hard heads had collided.

"And how's your head?"

"That might take longer to heal." She couldn't draw her

hand away as, ever so slowly, his eyelids lowered over a glittery wildfire of want.

"Ready to rock and roll?"

Quinn's booming voice brought them apart with a guilty jump. He was grinning widely as he approached with his ambling cowboy strut. His good-natured smile tightened as he looked between them, catching the combustible residue of their emotions.

"Got room for an extra passenger?"

Quinn responded to Xander's question with a hoist of his shaggy brows. "Mel, you wanting to do some sightseeing? Or is it just too damn hard to stay away from me?"

Her crude retort made him laugh out loud.

"Sure, darlin'. If only it was possible. Welcome aboard." And he waved his hand toward the hangar doors to where his DeHavilland Twin Otter was waiting. "Soon as I drop some of the boys off, I've got to deliver some supplies on a long line. Should be plenty of excitement for one morning. Which is a good thing, seeing as how I have such a headache." He pushed back the straw Stetson he was wearing to reveal a knot the size of an egg sunnyside up on his brow. He grinned at Xander. "Didn't think there was anyone with a head harder than mine. C'mon, son. You can sit up front and I'll give you the ten-cent tour."

That left Mel to climb in back with the half-dozen smoke jumpers he was transporting. She knew them all by name and they exchanged greetings with the spare words of gladiators girding up for their moment of glory. And as she strapped in as cargo instead of crew, she chafed at her own uselessness, at the stiff pride that wouldn't allow her to back down and get back to work.

And she stewed over the unlikely camaraderie she could see developing between Xander and Quinn as he went through an explanation of what they were doing and why, while her client nodded and asked good questions. And she suffered a pins-and-needles nervousness each time Xander glanced back from his co-pilot's seat without meaning to and his dark stare touched upon her. Quick glimpses that probably didn't signify anything but got her so stirred up, she found it hard to sit still as they lifted off into the searingly blue sky toward the smoke-smudged horizon.

From his front-row seat, Xander's sense of awe massed like the smoke clouds as they crested the ring of mountains protecting Reno and aimed for the forest lands beyond.

"Where are we headed?"

Quinn gestured off to his left where the ground glowed a hot, fiery red. "We'll be kicking these boys out right in front of that line and they're going to do their damnedest to keep it from advancing any farther. You done any jumping?"

"Some. Into a nice open field. Not into something like that and not at low altitude."

Quinn nodded at the sensibility of that. "These ol' boys are crazy. They can't wait to jump out of an airplane in some of the worst weather you've ever seen. Into some of the wildest areas you'd never want to go to just to square off against the dragon with nothing but hand tools. Like I said, crazy." But the respect in his tone was unmistakable. "Just giving them a lift this morning to replace the fellas that have been holding the line for the last thirty-two hours so's they can get some sleep and some grub and wash the smoke off before they get back to it. They love the jump but once they're on the ground, they're like any other firefighter making a living." He nodded toward the back. "Want to give it a go?"

For one pulse-hopping moment, the answer flared bright in his eyes.

Quinn laughed, shaking his head. "You would, wouldn't you?"

Reining in hard, Xander smiled thinly. "No, of course not."

"Bull. You're just a wild boy in a suit, aren't you, Alex."

Alex. He looked away, features grim, voice very soft and hardly audible over the engines. "That's not who I am anymore."

"Too bad. Think I would have liked you then."

Xander said nothing. He didn't need Quinn Naylor or the Parrishes or any of the men in back to like him. He wasn't here to make friends. But there was something about these people with their raw energy, their live-life-on-the-edge mentality, that drew him the way nothing else had for a long, long while. Would Alex Caufield have jumped out of the back into a forest fire? Hell, yes. Without blinking an eye. Would he have made fierce, passionate love to a woman in a bar bathroom? In a heartbeat. Because that's who he'd been. A wild boy, fearless, self-indulgent and self-absorbed. And that's why his life had gone straight to hell. That's why he couldn't go to visit his stepfather even though it was killing him by degrees not to.

They reached the jump zone, a flaming patch of ground right out of Dante's *Inferno*. Holding altitude at a low 1,500 feet, Quinn made a slow pass to give them the best possible chance for a safe landing. Land in the wrong spot, like on the other side of a ridge, and they'd spend the better part of a day hiking back to the fire, failing in their objective of immediate suppression. Land in the fire, itself, and they might not jump again. Ever.

Mel stood at the open door, seeing each one of them out with a smile and a thumbs-up. Watching her, Xander couldn't keep the sudden thrust of emotion from hamstringing his determined resolve. And when he settled back into his seat as the door slid shut, he couldn't help but notice Quinn Naylor's narrowed eyes, watching him watching Mel.

"Well, they're off to earn their pocket change," Quinn remarked at last to cut the sudden tension between them. "Helluva way to make a living."

"What about you? What's in this for you?"

Quinn gave him a shrewd look. "I'll tell you my story if you'll tell me yours." Then he laughed at the way Xander's expression closed down tight. "I thought so. Son, any fool can see there's more to you than meets the eye. I just haven't figured out what that is yet."

"Just making a living."

Naylor snorted. "Yeah, right. Nine to five to pay the bills? I don't think so. You don't have the look of someone who's ever had to punch a clock to get by. You got too much edge and attitude to work for someone else. And too many expensive hobbies."

"I don't have to work. I like to work."

Quinn smiled at his testy reply. "Sure. And I like to pay taxes about as much as I can see you liking to tote around a briefcase full of someone else's valuables, paying for protection when you could probably rip the spleen outta anybody who thought to—how did you put it—get in your face? Maybe Mel buys into that fiction, but I don't. Whatcha up to, Xander? Tell me you're not making trouble for me or my friends."

Chapter 9

"**I**'m not making trouble for anyone." That was no lie. They'd made their own trouble. It had nothing to do with him.

Quinn regarded him suspiciously for a long moment then told him, "My daddy was a wildcatter in Texas. My mama and me and my sisters grew up in the worst sort of place with nothing but heat and dirt and poor. And all I dreamed of was being surrounded by cool and green and rich. Knew I didn't want to work the rigs with my daddy but wasn't sure what else might be out there until I saw my first wildfire when I was nine. The minute I sucked in that smoke and breathed out excitement, I was hooked. And when I got a chance to go up in an airplane for twenty dollars at a county fair, I knew how I wanted to do it. Like an archangel swooping down out of heaven into the mouth of hell." He grinned. "My mama was a preacher's daughter."

Xander returned the contagious smile without thinking. Then he cautioned himself not to get caught up by the lazy drawl and rustic charm. Quinn Naylor was every bit as suspect as the Parrishes. He had everything—opportunity, knowledge, ability—that the Parrishes did. All he lacked was motive.

"Where's your family now?"

"Still in Texas." His expression quieted. "My daddy passed a few years back in an accident on the rig. My baby sis and my mama are looking out for her folks now that they're up there in years. My oldest sister is trying to raise a passel of kids on her own after her no-good husband took off and my middle sister, who got my share of the family brains, is at A&M making us damned proud. And I'm taking care of all of 'em as best I can."

Motive. One that left a sour taste and made Xander long to rinse and spit.

"What about your people, Alex? Where are your roots?"

His response came quick and easy, surprising him. "My mother doesn't have any. She follows the party crowd around the globe. Her father isn't a preacher. He's in the music business and she's what you might call his talent scout." And she'd been on the road, checking out that young, raw talent ever since he could remember. It wasn't a story he was particularly fond of telling, because he always felt he should make excuses for his mother's behavior, not because his audience was uncomfortable, but because he was. "I traveled with her when I was old enough. She thought it important for me to gain an international perspective on life. I would have settled for dirt-poor and in one place."

Quinn gave him an odd look. "No, you wouldn't. Trust me on that one. And your daddy?"

"My stepfather is in Colorado."

"And your real daddy?"

"I have no idea who he might be."

Quinn's pitying glance cut to the soul, the kind a man with deep roots gave the tumbleweed orphan of the entertainment business. And in that brief intuitive look, remarkably, Quinn Naylor saw right past the pedigree and the money to the loneliness of Xander's life. Giving him a shock of alarm. He was talking too much. And that was disturbing to someone who never betrayed anything of a personal nature to anyone. He quickly turned from introspective topics to the business at hand, gesturing down to the scorched earth below.

"Not much left, is there?"

"Ash and heartache for them that's got money and love sunk in. Takes a lifetime right down to the ground."

"Makes me wonder, being in my business, if someone wanted to hide something, like a crime, if a fire like this one would be the best way to cover the evidence."

Quinn's brow lowered, giving it thought. "Can't see much surviving that kind of a cleansing. But what kind of sick SOB would destroy so much to get away with something like that?"

"Someone with everything to gain and nothing to lose. Or someone paid by that someone."

"Arson, you mean? We hear of it sometimes. Crazies with a grudge aren't as common as just plain carelessness. But something always turns up to point the finger. It's not that easy to start a forest on fire and get it to do what you want. You have to understand the beast. How it thinks, how it eats. The average joe doesn't know those things and they make mistakes."

"But a professional?"

"Yeah. They'd know how to stoke its appetite and send it in the right direction." Then his narrowed gaze cut to Xander. "This fire was started by some campers in California who let their weenie roast get out of control. They've already given statements. Are you thinking it might be something else?"

"No, of course not. Just making conversation. The fire that burned Karen Parrish, did they ever find out what caused that one?"

"Bad luck and a shift in the wind." His pleasant drawl sharpened. "Don't try making it into something other than that or I will get in your face. The Parrishes are the closest thing to family I've got out here. You mess with them, you hurt any of them, I'll make you regret it."

Wisely, Xander said nothing.

"Tour's over. I've got work to do up here. Take a seat in back and tell Mel to get the long line ready."

Without comment, Xander unbuckled and worked his way back to the body of the plane. Mel greeted him with a cynical smile.

"Bored so soon?"

"He got bored with my conversation."

Mel's gaze followed his drop into a seat opposite hers. "You must have been using big words. He hates that."

Quinn loved an audience and it wasn't like him to chase away a captive one. Xander had done something to step on the toes of his snakeskin Tony Lama's and put him in a disagreeable coil. Unless Quinn's alpha-dog standing was threatened. She held to her smirk. Then a disconcerting thought. Had they been discussing her? A strange sensation quivered in her belly somewhere between alarm and annoyance. Then Xander smacked her back to reality with his quiet claim.

"I asked him about the fire that took your mother."

She sucked a pained breath then her expression closed down tight. "What do you want to know?" The question cut like gravel on the knees.

"I was asking if they knew how the fire started."

"And you were wondering why he might take offense at your idle interest in my family's misery?" She hated the glassy dampness that rimmed her lashes, blinking it away.

"No." His voice lowered to the husky rumble that rubbed across her raw mood like the sumptuous rasp of velvet. "I wanted to understand you better."

Her heart made a fearful lunge, almost escaping over the high-barred corral of her caution. "I'm not that complicated."

His lips compressed in a thin smile. "Oh, I think you are."

Not sure if she should be flattered or panicked, she didn't have the good sense to leave it alone. To leave him alone. "We were going to meet my father. The wind shifted. She died. Karen's in a wheelchair. Charley scorched his lungs going in for them. Paddy never got over the shock of it. I couldn't stop any of it from happening. And just what else are you dying to know?"

"I want to know why you're so afraid."

"Afraid? I'm not afraid of anything."

But he wasn't buying into her bluster. His solemn stare

pierced right to the heart of her, pinning her like a moth to a collection board. "You're afraid of the fire. Understandably so. And you're afraid of me. Why?"

"I am...not."

"Then come over here and sit with me."

She threw off her seat belt and crossed the safety barrier to settle on the cushions at his side. Their knees touched. They were close enough for her to see the startling green depths in his eyes. "Okay, I'm here. What's your point?"

His fingertips touched lightly to her cheek. She reared back so suddenly, her head knocked against the seat rest, her eyes wide and a little wild.

"You just made it for me."

To prove him wrong, she took hold of his hand, pressing his wrapped palm to the side of her face while her fierce glare challenged him. His expression remained inscrutable as she dragged his fingertips across the firm line of her lips then traced them down her neck to the open vee of her camp shirt. The instant they reached the swell of her breast, she felt his resistance, subtle at first, becoming a power struggle against further advancement. Her expression grew mocking.

"It's you who's afraid of me."

He didn't refute it, altering her smug victory into a unsettling truce. The instant she released his hand, he pulled away.

"Buckle in for landing," Quinn hollered back, giving them the excuse to retreat warily. The descent was fast, the landing rough enough to distract them and then Teddy was yanking up the cargo door, yelling, "Mel, help me get the line hooked on."

She was out of her seat in a fast second, leaving Xander off balance and out of sorts. He didn't like being rattled from his complacency. It wasn't good business. It wasn't safe and it wasn't smart.

And his palms grew damp as he considered how soft and firm and pliant she would have felt if he'd allowed her to move his hand just a little lower.

"You can c'mon back up if you like," Quinn called.

As the mercurial Quinn was preferable to the dangers of lingering in back with his emotions exposed, Xander returned to the co-pilot's seat to silently watch Quinn fussing with his gauges. As he fidgeted with his shoulder harness, Quinn mentioned casually, "If you think you matter a damn to her, you're mistaken."

Covering his surprise, Xander asked, "Why would I think that?"

"I know the look. I've seen it enough times."

"Just how many times would that put between you and me?"

Quinn stiffened. "Enough for me to warn you again that you're nothing special. She's great on the windup but lousy at the follow-through. Just some friendly advice."

"Is that what we are? Friends?"

An angry glance slanted to assess Xander's unapproachable facade. "No. I guess not. My mistake."

"Quinn," Teddy shouted from the back. "Cargo's ready. Sheridan wants to know if you'll pick up some hotshots and give them a lift."

"Tell him sure thing. The meter will be running." He noticed Xander starting to stand and waved him back into the seat. "You might as well ride first class, Mr. Big Shot. Something tells me you're used to having the best seat in the house. You don't get that coming from dirt and poor."

They spent the day in a constant shuttle between the supply camps and hot spots, dropping off men, meals and a boost of morale. Quinn was, just as Charley ascribed, a fine pilot, zipping in and out of the fire so close Xander swore his nose hairs had been singed. And while they were doing that, daring the flames to catch them, all Xander could think of was Mel in the back, cloaked by the denial of her fears, suffering them alone, too stubborn to look to anyone else for support.

By the time they took a break for a hot meal at one of the mobile wilderness kitchens, darkness had begun to seep in, layering across the ground and silently building toward the treetops. While he chatted with the crewmen he knew, at least by sight, and helped dish them up their meals as they stood almost dead on their feet, from the corner of his eyes Xander could see Mel unraveling. On the ground, so close to the stench of smoke and threat of flames, a haunted look shadowed her expression even as her mood geared up into a bunch of raw nerves. She nearly vibrated with a kinetic anxiousness. Her jumpy tension made the others nervous and Quinn worry. And Xander understood why the other pilot would consider her a danger in the sky. She was an open wound of anxiety and undirected anger, snapping at all who approached without knowing why. And he ached for her, knowing what it was like to struggle with fear when all alone.

It was late when they finally headed back for Reno. Teddy rode up front with Quinn giving Xander no place to go but in the back. Cautiously, he approached Mel where she sat in the second row of double seats, staring out the window at the glow beneath them. She glanced up at him, her expression carefully guarded.

"Mind if I sit?"

"Help yourself."

To anything? To everything? If only he could. He settled for taking the seat beside her.

In the darkness, with the drone of the twin Pratt & Whitney turbines creating a soothing white noise, Mel tried to let go of the frenetic energy bunching inside her. Her heart still jackhammered, her breathing labored. Her muscles remained knotted and quivering with no means of relief in sight.

It was the smell of smoke. It curled seditiously about her senses bringing with it the whisper of an old dread. As it teased her nostrils, she could hear the echo of screams inside her head, within those memories that she might hide but could never escape. Those horrible sounds of pain and blame.

"Mel, don't leave me!"

She squeezed her eyes shut tight, willing the awful sights and sounds away. Wishing away the repeated nightmare vision that came to her in dreams, of the fire devil wearing Karen's face.

Xander eased his arm in a casual drape about her shoulders, just letting it rest there in a comfortable, comforting weight, inviting her to take whatever she might need from him. Feeling her tremble, he let his fingers run lightly up and down her sleeve in a gesture meant to calm, but instead, managed to kink her nerves up even tighter.

"Don't," she growled, beginning to shrug off his support

then contrarily clutching at his hand, curling him more closely about her. For a moment, she relaxed, gratefully soaking up the solid heat of him. And it was heaven. But all too soon, the coil of agitation returned, feeding her restlessness, provoking her anxiety. It was the scent of ash and destruction that clung to his clothing. The sense of safety was gone. She couldn't sit still. She had to be doing something to work off the tension or she'd explode.

The flat of her hand rested on the firm wall of his abdomen. A determined inch of her fingers coaxed the hem of his T-shirt free so her palm could push up under it. She skimmed over the warm stretch of skin, riding the rugged six-pack contours like challenging moguls on a motocross course. Down to the waistband of his jeans. Letting her fingertips race along the edge of that barrier as if it was a retaining wall for his passions. A dangerous ride at such breakneck speed.

"Don't," he warned quietly, catching her hand, intending to tuck it someplace safe, then contrarily placed it atop his straining zipper. His breath shuddered as she closed about him.

There was nothing gentle or hesitant in the way she touched him, stroking, at first through denim and then, upon hot flesh. Her hand squeezed, her nails scraped and he was pressing back against his seat, his heels digging into the floor, spikes of sensation robbing him of coherent thought. And all too soon he was excruciatingly aware of just how long he'd existed in his monkish state. Far too long to endure much more of her determined fondling with any degree of success.

"Mel, stop," he whispered hoarsely, barely hanging on to the ragged edge of his self-control.

He glanced toward the front of the cabin, through the doorway, to where he was sure Quinn and Teddy would be alerted by his abnormally loud breathing. He could hear the murmur of their voices, both blissfully ignorant of what was going on in the darkness behind them as they continued to talk baseball.

He reached down to extract Mel's hand and preserve the illusion that he had a little more self-restraint than a fourteen-year-old boy viewing his first porn site. He managed a salvaging breath then forgot all about time and place and any objection as her head lowered to his lap. His hand fisted in her bright hair meaning to pull her up, then holding her there as she licked along the hard length of him, briefly flirting with the swirl of her tongue before taking him with her hungry, devouring mouth. And there was nothing delicate or leisurely in the way she drew him to a fierce, shattering conclusion. His head banged back against the seat. He saw stars, then was rocketing amongst them. Only then, when he was panting, drained and dazed in the aftermath, did she allow him any degree of tenderness. A soft kiss, a light caress before zipping him back up. She didn't return to her seat, instead pillowing her head in his lap, her arm hugging about his knees.

"What are we going to do about this, Xander?"

He couldn't find his voice. So she answered for him.

"I say we finish it so we can get back to some kind of normal function. I need to get my life back and I can't until I get you out of my system."

She made her emotions sound like some unpleasant affliction in need of purging. Not exactly flattering considering the splendid, will-sapping gift she'd just given him. But he understood her fear and agreed. She relaxed with a sigh, her bones seeming to liquify. He touched her hair with an unsteady hand as emotions even less stable ricocheted within the walls of his chest. He could hear Kyle's advice, as his friend flung his own arrogance back into his face. *Screw her before she screws you over*. That was exactly what it was going to take if he was going to finish what he needed to do.

By the time Quinn brought them down with a light touch to the tarmac in Reno, they were both operating under a tight-reined control. With quick thank-yous to their pilot that left Quinn frowning suspiciously, they went to Mel's Jeep and she wheeled them toward the hotel like an Indy driver. As they crossed the noisy lobby, Mel clung to the bend of Xander's elbow, clutching so she wouldn't lose her nerve. He'd been right. She was afraid of him, afraid of what this might lead to if they weren't extremely careful. When she dared risk a glance up at him, the sight of his immobile profile gave her strength. If he could keep it under control, so could she. And once they'd exhausted their every curiosity, she could go home to her own bed alone, free of this desperate need to know. To know what it would be like with a man she might have been able to love.

They rode up in the elevator with a half-dozen others, forcing them to stand close. Xander's hand touched lightly to the small of her back. Hers was gripping the back pocket of his jeans. She was suddenly shaking, not sure at all this was such a good idea but wanting him so much, so desperately, she knew there was no going back.

Murmuring a polite, "Excuse me," Xander guided her out of the elevator and into the empty hallway. He fumbled with his key card, inserting it once, twice before a charmed number three gave them the green light. And as he turned her inside his darkened room, his arm scooped about her waist and his head began to lower in search of her lips. He froze at the press of her fingertips against his mouth.

"No," she told him with an unexpected soberness. "Things can't get that involved. It's just sex, Xander." Then more hesitantly, "All right?"

He paused then straightened. And she didn't know whether to be relieved or regretful when he said softly, "All right."

To distract herself from breaking her own edict, Mel began to hurriedly strip off her clothes while Xander did the same. She went to crawl up onto his bed, across the taut cover that had stirred her fantasies, not looking back as he followed more slowly, stopping at the nightstand to withdraw the protection they'd overlooked in their previous hurry. Feigning calm, she watched him take the proper precautions before coming down to join her. There was nothing reckless about him now, not that that made the sight of him, all sleek, hard and impressively virile, any less exciting. His features were cut into dramatically shadowed highs and lows, dark, beautiful. Emotionless. His body was sculpted perfection, breathtaking. He layered over her, holding himself up on elbows and toes so that they were parallel but not touching while his cool, dark stare penetrated her own. She'd said she didn't want to attach any meaning to what was happening between them but hadn't realized just how difficult he was going to make that just by being close enough for her to feel his body heat without the scorch of passion.

Twining her legs about his, she rolled abruptly to come up astride him. With a quick lift and settling of her hips, she'd taken him inside her. Pausing to appreciate the way he, again, filled her with such sure and almost frightening power. She heard his breath suck in sharply as his hands clutched her knees, relaxed, just resting atop them. His eyes were closed. His features revealed nothing beyond a gorgeously composed exterior. Wondering what it would take to shake him from that frustrating calm, she rose up and slid back onto him by agonizingly slow increments. The dark crescent of his lashes flickered then lay still. She could hear his soft, steady breathing.

Was he thinking about baseball? Whatever he was concentrating on, it wasn't her. And suddenly just sex was very lonely business.

Through slitted eyes, Xander watched her as she rode him with the sinuous grace and generic sexiness of a pole dancer in an exotic lounge. It gave him the same restless, voyeuristic urgency he'd experienced in the bar. Forbidden and untouchable, she moved above him, setting her own pace, intent on a taking pleasure, excluding him except as the means to a solitary end. He shut out that sight so he could focus on the hot intensity pooling low and fierce. Just get it done and let her leave. Don't make it personal. Then the razor's edge of tension would be gone and he could get back to work.

Her breathing grew low and labored. How would she look in these final seconds? Just imagining sent emotions arrowing through him too swift and complex to identify. Dangerous, deep, scary emotions. To hide from them, all he had to do was keep his eyes closed until the moment passed. But he couldn't.

The sight of her hit him like a defibrillator to the heart.

He must have said her name, because she looked at him with a dazed sort of surprise and recognition before her lovely features registered a dazzling kaleidoscope of responses from tension to wonder to a lusciously hedonistic relief. After a lengthy shudder, she went limp, slumping above him, sagging upon the brace of her forearms atop his chest. The only thing holding her up could have been the strength of his erection.

She sighed with a luxurious contentment.

No. No, no, no, no, no.

Too late. He was so in love with this wildly unpredictable woman, he couldn't stand not acting on it. Telling her outright, of course, would be out of the question. An unforgivable betrayal of his professional ethics. That left him with no other choice.

"I'm sorry."

She misunderstood. In a breathless little voice that wound about his chest to squeeze with a crushing ferocity, she murmured. "I'm sorry, too. I waited for you as long as I could. I'm a bit out of practice. It's been almost a year since…I made a mistake then by jumping into something I shouldn't have and I didn't want to make another one with you."

The flicker of a smile escaped then he was all quiet intensity once more. "I'm sorry, Mel."

"It *was* a mistake, wasn't it?" Her features crumpled briefly then assumed a desperate bravado. "I'm sorry, too, Xander."

He caught her by the shoulders, holding her in place. She could feel him pulse inside her with a demanding power that quite frankly terrified her.

"I'm sorry, Mel. Things are about to get very, very involved. And it's not going to be just sex."

Before she could shake her head, his hands came up to clasp her face between them, drawing her down for a kiss so long and sweet and soul stirring that, when he allowed her to lift away, her vision was skewed by tears.

"I can't do this, Xander. I can't."

His thumbs sketched tenderly over her cheeks, stemming the sudden embarrassing trickle of dampness. "I'll do it, Mel. I'll take all the risks. All you have to do is let me."

Her fingertips trembled against his strong jaw. Her resolve wobbled.

"Let me make love to you, Melody. I want to hear you say my name. Say my name."

"Alex," she whispered with a heartbreaking vulnerability. "Alex, love me."

He almost said, I do.

There was nothing dramatic, nothing fiercely claiming or primal in the way he won her passions over. Just more of the searingly slow and steady conquest of her reluctant heart and soul. He rolled up over her, kissing her with an unhurried thoroughness that had her panting in impatience. But he refused to be rushed, lingering upon her lips as if he had a lifetime to learn each unique curve and swell. As if the taste of her held an exquisite reward he'd been yearning for. She was shivering by the time he eased back to assess his effect on her, finding her pleasantly shattered.

"Alex." She breathed his name and he kissed her again,

letting passion stir and escalate in an unstoppable tide. She moaned softly, her torso rising to offer her breasts. After charting their fullness with his fingertips, he lowered his head. His mouth moved with a maddening attentiveness, teasing with the graze of his teeth, laving those sensitive tips with the wet rasp of his tongue until she was restlessly threading her fingers through his hair. Until a piercingly direct suction dragged helpless cries from her with ropes of glassy fire.

He slid down the length of her body, his mouth and warm breath scorching along her skin until she was strung tight with anticipation. He paused for an instant to let her expectation build to an almost shattering degree before parting her like a silk-lined jewel case, his mouth seeking the pearl within. Finding it with the probe of his tongue. Rolling that treasure between his lips, tugging with his teeth until her legs began to tremble. She made soft mewling sounds and twisted her fingers in his hair tight enough to make his eyes water. But he continued determinedly, driving her to an explosive climax. The last of those fierce spasms clutched at him as he seated himself deep inside her once again and began to move.

Mel gave herself over to the open mouthed kisses that prowled recklessly over her cheeks, her nose, her chin before settling for a long, plunging tangle with her tongue. Afraid she was going to tear his hair out by the roots, she dropped her hands to his shoulders, kneading there in a frantic rhythm. Never, ever, did she expect her wonderfully sated body to respond with another seismic quickening. Taken by surprise, she arched up against him only to have his hands catch her hips, anchoring her there to meet his hard, driving thrusts. Pleasure burst with her wild, keening cry of his name and he came hurtling after.

Finally, he was able to shift his weight off her, settling to one side because she still held to him too frantically for him to leave the tight circle of her arms. Not that he wanted to. As he stroked back the tousle of her hair, he discovered she was weeping. Not a delicate little sniffle but great gulping sobs that tore his conscience in two. When he said her name, she turned huge shimmering eyes to him, their depths rich with a miserable contentment. Before he could ask what was wrong, knowing the answer because that same paralyzing fear clenched about his own heart, she trapped his face between her hands and pulled him to her for a long, rather desperate kiss, searching for the means to hold on to this fiercely tender moment without compromising everything else. She pushed him back to anxiously search his unguarded stare, her heart laid bare.

"I don't want to need you. I don't want to need anyone."

"I'm sorry," he said again before sinking back in her kiss. Then, simply holding her close. Gradually, as her passions and fears quieted, she began to touch him, tentatively following the enticing swells of his shoulder and upper arm, tracing the unlikely art of his tribal armband while that light overture knotted him up inside. Then her hand rested upon his chest.

"Alex." Parting hung heavy in that single word.

"Mel, don't go. I don't want to need you, either, but I do. Right now, I do. Stay with me."

Her hand skimmed around his ribs, lying flat upon his back until they were pressed close. And after a time, they both let down their wary guards to relax. And finally sleep.

A buzzing rumble woke Mel some hours later. She opened her eyes, disoriented then entranced by the sight of a naked Alex Caufield stretched out beside her all gloriously buff and endearingly serene in slumber. The obnoxious sound came from the vibration of her cell phone atop his wooden nightstand. Dragging her attention from him, she fumbled for her phone.

"This better be a world-crisis-ranked emergency," she growled softly as Xander stirred lazily amid the tangle of bedcovers. They hadn't found their way under the sheets yet.

"Mel, where are you?"

"Karen? I was asleep. What is it?" Her hesitation went on just long enough to alert Mel. "Karen?"

"It's Xander Caufield, Mel. He's not who you think he is."

Chapter 10

He caught the glint of movement out of the corner of his eye. A reflexive twist of his body kept him from taking a direct hit to the head from the flying steel courier case. He cursed in startlement and pain as it deflected off his shoulder.

Mel Parrish stood at the foot of the bed, dressed and furious while he was wearing nothing but his bewilderment and the beginnings of a spectacular bruise.

"What the hell is this about?" he demanded. Horribly afraid he already knew.

She jabbed a finger at the case where it lay in villainy upon the floor. "Open it."

"What?"

"There's no point in it, is there? We both know it's empty. As empty as your soul. I can't believe I let you—" She broke off to grab desperately for a breath of composure.

Then she was all cold business again. "You come around me or my family again, I'll tear out your cold heart with my bare hands."

The same way he'd just torn out hers.

She wouldn't cry. She wouldn't let him know how deeply, perhaps mortally she was wounded. But at least he had enough respect for her not to try to drag the pretense out any farther.

"How did you find out?" ·

"Karen. She made a routine call on that check you wrote her because of the amount. You're not employed by Western Mutual Insurance. They retained you as a mercenary to do whatever it took to recover their money for them. Is this what you decided it would take, Alex? Or is it Xander? You used me. You used my family, my friends." Her voice lowered a tremulous octave. "You son of a bitch. You had me believing you were something special. I thought—" She broke off with a jerky swallow and let her anger take over again as she told him flatly, "You are very, very good at your job."

As the door shut behind her, it took Xander precious seconds to break from his dismayed stupor. Then he was rolling from the bed, stubbing his toe on the offending case, snatching up the first thing he could find to put on so he could race after her. He thrust his arm between the closing elevator doors and pushed them apart. Mel was flattened against the rear of the car, her stark features wet with tears. Seeing him, her temper blew up like a thunderstorm.

"Leave me alone," she shrieked at him, coming close enough to stab frantically at the Close Door button.

"Mel, listen to me."

"Why? So you can tell me another lie?"

He wedged himself in the doorway, noticing for the first time a group of three elderly women regarding him with wide, appreciative eyes, standing there in his briefs. He paid them no further attention.

"Mel, I was hired by the insurance company to find out who was setting fires to make fraudulent claims. A man died and another one, an innocent one, is in prison. The facts brought me here, to you, your family, your friends. I'm just trying to uncover the truth. I'm trying to find a criminal."

"And just who do you think that is? Me?"

He didn't answer at first, tragedy darkening his expression to a tortuous degree.

"Who? Quinn?"

Finally, he took a small breath and answered softly. "Your uncle, with or without your father's help."

Her slap knocked him back a step but he still held on to the door to persist. "Ask Charley where the money came from to pay for Karen, for the gambling debts."

"You're wrong, Xander. You are wrong."

"I'm not and you know it, too."

She struck him again, harder, but not as hard as he deserved. Nothing could deal out a brutal enough blow to offset his betrayal. He made one last petition.

"Mel, the man in prison is my father."

That jerked her up short but only for a heartbeat.

"I don't care."

Her fist pounded on his injured hand and, with a gasp, he let go and the doors shut between them.

While he stood in the hall, nursing his throbbing hand, a foursome of conventioneers bent on gambling came around the corner and stopped to stare at him in his lack of clothing.

"What are you looking at?" he snarled with enough distilled menace to send them scrambling for the stairs.

Why hadn't he listened to Kyle? Why hadn't he followed his own dictates that said don't get involved. Don't ever get involved. Why hadn't he paid attention to Mel when she tried to back away from what he *knew* would end up in disaster? He'd all but forced her into a level of intimacy far beyond safe and acceptable. And while he'd never promised not to hurt her, he'd let her believe he could be trusted.

And while he was at it, he should have taken care to guard his own heart.

He stopped at his door and reached for his pocket. Finding only bare hip. He was in his underwear without the benefit of pockets. Or a key.

About that time, a maid backed out of one of the neighboring rooms carrying a handful of towels. She stopped and stared. With his most charming smile, he called, "I seem to have locked myself out. Would you happen to have a passkey?"

Her eyes filled with angry tears, Mel wheeled out of the hotel lot heading, not home, but to Karen's for comfort. She left the Jeep on the tarmac, hopping into the Long Ranger and firing it up. The routine checks kept her distracted for long enough to get her emotions under a shaky control, then she was popping up and scooting off toward the south end of Lake Tahoe where her cousin owned a small single-story home with attached studio. She also had a nice landing square free of power lines in the field across the road available anytime Mel wanted to drop in for a chat, even after hours. After one look at Mel's pinched expression, Karen wheeled back to let her in and headed straight for the kitchen to get a bottle of wine.

Mel loved Karen's tiny place. It was neat, stylish and spotless, everything her own was not. It was her haven when she wanted to feel girlie and dish gossip and occasionally have her nails done. What she truly loved was the view. A large deck ran the length of it and it was that panoramic setting from which her cousin's creativity stemmed. The deep cold waters of the lake shimmered in the moonlight behind a stand of firs. Karen maintained an oasis of flowering plants that always seemed to be in bloom, drenching the evening with their perfume. She liked color and contrasting textures and calm, all the things Mel was missing. Karen often teased that her life ran on a linear plane more like a man's than a woman's circular highs and lows. Mel never minded much except at times like this when she needed to find a way off her straight-and-narrow path. And the one she was on was a definite dead end.

How had things gotten so out of control where Xander Caufield was concerned? What kind of man could wear another's skin so easily that even after it was shed, one disbelieved the truth of what he really was? The things he'd done, those acts of bravery on her behalf, on Teddy's. He'd put his very life on the line, for what? A bonus check?

His father.

A terrible pain twisted through her. It didn't matter. It couldn't matter. There was no excuse for the way he'd misused her. She closed her eyes, reliving his kisses. So convincing.

She heard the whir of Karen's chair from where she

stood leaning against the rail and took the glass of Merlot even though she preferred a cheap draft over the finest vintage.

"Want to talk?"

Her smile was bittersweet. "Maybe in a minute."

"Take your time." Then, contrarily she asked, "You were with him, weren't you?" At Mel's alarmed glance, she smiled and shrugged. "You smell like him. He wears a very nice cologne."

"I really liked him, Karen," she confessed miserably. "I thought he might be—"

"The one?"

She could only nod as her throat tightened around the weeping she still needed to get done.

"Didn't you think that about Quinn, too?"

"Quinn? No. Whatever gave you that idea? There was never anything between us except a good argument."

Karen seemed confused. "But you slept with him."

"When we were both too drunk to see straight after almost dying during a rescue. I hardly think that equates to love or anything like it."

"Oh."

"Besides," Mel added with a wry smile. "I thought you had a thing for that stubborn Texan."

"Me?" She blushed brightly. "We're just friends."

"Right. And that's why you run over my feet whenever he's in the room." She was quiet for a moment, then asked, "Karen, why didn't you have the follow-up surgeries so you could walk again and lead a normal life?"

Karen was silent for a moment, her features briefly twisting with emotion before becoming the serene canvas Mel was used to seeing. "I already do, Melody. I'm very happy with my life just the way it is. Besides, physical perfection doesn't equal a charmed life. Look at your mother."

Mel frowned slightly. What did her mother have to do with anything?

"She was beautiful, intelligent and lost her life foolishly chasing after a happiness she couldn't hold on to. Parrish women have always made bad choices when it comes to love." She held up her hand to halt the expected protest. "It was all over your face the first time you introduced him."

Mel gripped her lips tight then challenged, "And you're not hot for Quinn Naylor?"

"Like I said, bad choices. Quinn will never see me parked in your shadow. My mom deserted Charley and me to run off after a blackjack dealer with a slick smile. Yours was constantly trying to cover up for your Paddy's indiscretions. Not exactly great examples to follow."

"He lied to me, Karen." Those words stung, a raw wound.

"I know."

Something made Mel pull back from the complete truth. She glossed it over by saying, "About everything. About how he felt about me." Now that, she realized somewhat uncomfortably, was a lie. Xander had been honest about his feelings. He'd wanted her as much as she had him.

She set the nearly untouched glass down on one of the mosaic-topped tables her cousin had scattered about the patio. "Thanks for the wine and for letting me whine."

"Do you have to go so soon?"

Mel, don't go.

The spectacular scenery began to blur.

"Stay, Melody. Or do you have other plans?"

Not now. Tomorrow would be soon enough to confront Charley with Xander's crazy theories. It wasn't like she had a job waiting. It wasn't as if Xander would be waiting. And for all her trouble, she wasn't even sure she'd be paid.

She couldn't stop the sudden quiver of her jaw. The shivering just got bigger, seeping down to her hands, her knees, her heart until she was a useless mass of trembling. Karen's hand slipped inside hers, squeezing in support.

"You've always been there for me, Karen. We always have each other to count on when the going gets rough."

"If you can't trust family to be there for you, who can you trust? Don't cry over him, Mel. He wasn't worth it."

That was the problem. He was. He was everything she wanted, right down to the damnable family loyalty that allowed him to make love to her as part of his scheme to ruin her. Pretending to care for her because of his love for his father. She understood that kind of protectiveness. She just didn't know how she was going to survive it.

She had no clearer idea when she got up with the dawn, scenting the scorch of the fire on the incoming wind. She left a note for Karen, thanking her for once again being there to help her hold it all together. Then she headed home, to face the threatened collapse of all she held dear.

What collapsed was her will the moment she walked into her room to find the wrapped painting propped against her dresser. She tore the paper from the front and stood staring at the sunset until the pallet of colors all ran together before her eyes.

She heard footsteps behind her and for one more-than-foolish moment, her heart catapulted up into her throat. But it wasn't Xander's husky voice that greeted her.

"Do you think we're going to wait all day? Get that bird gassed up and ready to go. You got a crew waiting."

She stared at Quinn as if he'd lost his mind.

"Do you want to work or don't you? I don't know what strings your fancy boyfriend pulled, but he got you back under contract and in the air. That fire ain't gonna just sit there until you feel good and ready to go. Get a move on, girl."

The flat of his hand slapped against her rump, startling her into motion. "Fuel her up for me, Quinn, while I get changed."

"What is it about women? Always got to worry about what they're wearing."

She flung her arms about Quinn Naylor's neck and squeezed hard, not caring that he was the one who'd grounded her in the first place. Not seeing his expression crumple in an instant of bittersweet devotion. Because Quinn knew why Caufield had used his considerable wealth to go over his head.

Xander had done it because he and Mel were lovers.

Kyle D'Angelo eyed his friend warily. He'd arrived at the ungodly hour of five in the morning needing a shave and coffee. The fact that he had his eyes open, let alone that his stare was razor sharp, was odd enough. He was wearing a sinfully expensive Armani suit coat over a hooded sweat jacket and faded jeans. And high tops with dangling laces. Was this the Xander Caufield who never stepped into daylight without being immaculately groomed?

It was the woman, of course. But a friend wouldn't mention that fact.

"What's the matter? She kick you out of bed?"

With a look that could have hewn granite, Xander ignored the question to ask one of his own. "Have you heard from him again?"

"Last night. I'd left you several messages, but apparently you were otherwise occupied."

His cynical observation bought a leaner tension to Xander's already taut features. "Well, you have my full attention now."

"Are you sure?"

"Yes." That cut like the business edge of an ax.

"Okay." He shoved a mug of coffee into his friend's hand. "In two days for one-hundred grand."

"Two days." So soon. After all his searching, all his planning, all his scheming, in two days he'd have his reward. His vindication. At whose expense?

Noting his unexpected hesitation, Kyle asked quietly, "Are you ready for this, Xander?"

"Ready? Yes, of course." And he looked it. He had his game face back on and his gaze was flat black. Inanimate. Like a shark's. "Did you set it up the way we discussed?"

"A drop three hours before it's scheduled to go up in smoke. He'll pick the time then we'll get our people in place."

"I'll have the money here by tonight. Then all he has to do is take the bait." He paused then added, "We need to act fast. The plan might be compromised."

"What? How?"

"Mel Parrish knows why I'm here."

D'Angelo stared at him, aghast, disbelieving. "Did you just happen to share that with her in idle pillow talk?"

Xander's expression never flickered. "No. Her cousin did a background check on me. But as far as I know, they haven't made a connection between the two of us."

"As far as you know?" He swore softly. "You need to make yourself scarce until this goes down. No mistakes."

"I don't make mistakes."

His friend called him on that with a slight lift of his brows. How could he argue? He'd made a mistake with Mel. A huge, unprofessional, unexpected, unheard-of mistake. Now he had to make sure no one else paid the price for it. "I screwed up."

Knowing what that admission must have cost him, Kyle shrugged it off. "Get your stuff, quick and quiet, and get back here. No harm done if they think you were just sniffing around. Maybe it will rattle them into making some mistakes."

Them. The Parrishes.

"Alex, you know if it turns out to be her uncle, her family will be destroyed."

"Your point?" His ruthlessness made Kyle wince.

"That's not going to matter to you?"

"It's not my problem, Kyle."

"If you say so." His friend sounded sincere. He looked so emotionally detached, Kyle feared if he suggested they go out and strangle puppies, he'd have no objection to that either. So why didn't he believe it?

"I need to talk to my father."

Kyle covered his surprise. "We could be there by—"

"Just a phone call is fine, but I don't have the number."

It was a start. "I'll set it up."

"Thank you." He paused, then said much more softly, "Thank you, Kyle."

Studying the pressure-formed angles of his friend's face, Kyle D'Anglo feared when Xander broke, it was going to be a fissure of ice-age proportions.

He managed a few hours' sleep sprawled on one of the Adirondack lounges on the porch but felt no more rested when he woke. His nerves were guy-wire taut. His thoughts ticked with the precision of his expensive Swiss watch. Yet when Kyle brought him the phone, in a moment of absolute panic, Xander almost refused to take it. But of course, he didn't.

"Alex?"

The sound of his voice, the grateful, teary way Evan Sanders spoke his name, almost tore him down completely.

"I couldn't believe it when they told me. I'd almost given up hope— How are you, son?"

"One question."

"Anything."

"The truth."

"What do you need to know?"

"Are you guilty?"

A moment of silence, then his reply. "No, son. I'm not."

Xander squeezed his eyes shut, clutching the phone with both hands. They were shaking.

"Alex? Are you still there?"

"That's all I needed to know, Dad."

"No, it isn't. I love you, son. It wasn't your faul—"

Xander pressed the disconnect button, his forehead resting on the cell while his emotions pitched and yawed.

"How 'bout some breakfast?" came Kyle's cheery suggestion. "One of my exes taught me to make the perfect eggs Benedict."

Xander nodded, not looking up, unable to speak.

Kyle took the cell from him and touched his hand briefly to the back of his bowed dark head. "I make a wicked Bloody Mary."

Another faint nod.

Kyle gave his friend a push. "C'mon. You've got just enough time to grab a shower. Then we'll feast. Then we'll get down to business."

He was thinking about that business, and how it would affect those he'd come to know and respect…and more…over the past few days. Preoccupied, he didn't notice the other vehicle at first until he glanced in the rearview of his rental car to see the massive grill of the SUV looming up behind him. He increased his speed, putting a more comfortable distance between him and the other driver. After a few tight turns, the grill was back.

And then he felt the first bump. A nudge, but enough to have him struggling to retain control of the sleek Lexus.

He'd taken the eastern route around the lake, passing on the lush resort scenery as too peaceful for his mood in favor of the harsh landscape that led through Silver City. The barren slabs of gray rock suited his dark brooding. Usually when he left a job behind, he didn't feel one way or another about it. He couldn't say the same this time. Sneaking to the hotel to snatch up his bags and slink away without a word to anyone smacked of guilt and villainy. Rightfully so. He'd misused these good people. He'd represented himself as something he wasn't, someone they could like and trust and invite to join them. An envied place he'd never occupied before. He'd deceived them, then betrayed them. And he couldn't brush it off inconsequentially as an occupational hazard.

He cringed as he considered the companionable weight of Teddy Greenbaum's arm about his shoulders. When he recalled Quinn Naylor's drawling claim of "I would have liked you then," he realized glumly that there was nothing likable about him now. He'd enjoyed the rough-and-tumble fellowship in the bar, the chance to get dirty wrenching on an engine with Charley Parrish. Simple things, real things, things he'd lost touch with as he skirted the edges of other people's lives without living one of his own. And then there was Mel. He couldn't begin to think of her now without feeling the worst kind of coward. *You're very, very good at your job.* Yes, he was. Because it was all he had.

And that job had grown suddenly dangerous.

It could have been some redneck irritated by his overly cautious negotiating of the winding mountain road. Could have been but he didn't think so. Not after the second, more aggressive, kiss to his bumper sent the rental shimmying. He accelerated, dividing his attention between the road and the grill behind him. A sheer wall rose up on his left and a plunging drop-off threatened on his right. Nowhere to go except faster. He hadn't seen another car since leaving the old mining town, and the only one on the road with him was determined to knock him off it. And way out here, how long would it take for someone to find him, or rather what was left of him, if he went over the edge to make a abrupt, fatal stop at the abandoned quarry far, far below.

He took the next corner with tires shrieking, hanging on to his calm the way his vehicle was trying to stick to the blacktop. His heart hammering, his mouth as dry as his hands were wet, he concentrated on the hairpin turns until they crested the top and started down.

Down was worse.

Unable to brake sensibly because of the hulking monster trying to climb into his back seat, he rushed headlong at fifty then sixty plus. Metal screeched as he rubbed the rock wall, bouncing him out toward the open spaces. He fought the wheel, gravel churning the way his stomach was churning as the rear of the vehicle swung wide and nearly off the edge, crowded by the maniac in his rearview.

He was going to die before telling two important people that he was sorry. That he loved them.

And that was unacceptable.

Then he saw his chance. A scenic turnout rimming the next sharp curve. Just a car width of extra space, but maybe it would be enough.

He slammed on the brakes, shuddering into the outside lane, careening toward the optimistic safety of a guardrail that had no prayer of keeping him from hurtling into a two-hundred-foot free fall. He spun, crunching loose stone, headlight shattering from an impact that threw him into the steering wheel just as the air bag deployed. Unable to see where he was going, time stood still for a long moment. Then the car rocked to a stop. He heard the other vehicle roar past him over the pulse beats thundering in his head.

Pinned back into his seat, just trying to get control of his breathing, he got another shock as the door to the Lexus was yanked open. Trapped and helpless, he closed his eyes as a quick thought stabbed through his mind.

Mel, I'm sorry. I didn't mean to hurt you. I—

"Oh, my God! Are you all right?"

A woman's voice. He felt her tug at his shoulder belt.

"That guy was crazy. I thought he was going to push you right over the side."

You and me, both.

Struggling past the air bag, he was finally able to slide out of the car and onto his rump in the still-smoking gravel. He put his head between his knees as everything spun, breathing deep until the urge to throw up gradually passed.

"Are you okay? I have a cell phone. Should I call the police? An ambulance?"

He glanced up at the ashen-faced woman and beyond her to the soccer-mom mobile and two frightened kids peering out from the rear seat. "No, I'm okay," he managed to wheeze, trying to ease her fear with a wobbly smile. "I could use a ride back to Reno."

For the next forty minutes, he sat shaking in the passenger seat, listening happily to them yammer on and on about inconsequential things because he was still alive to be their captive audience. It took a half hour for the sports drink they gave him to stop roiling in his stomach, threatening to come back up every time they eased gingerly around a turn. He didn't question the wisdom of giving the driver Mel's address instead of going to the hotel. He needed to see who was home. And if there was a steaming SUV parked in the vicinity.

"Are you sure you're all right?"

He smiled at the Good Samaritan because he knew without a doubt if she and her family hadn't come upon him when they did, he'd be dead. He had a scrap of paper with her name and address shoved into his pocket. She'd had to write it because his hand was so unsteady the letters were illegible. To thank the single mother, he'd have a college fund set up for her kids.

"I'm fine. Really. Thank you, again."

Reassured, she smiled and waved as she drove off, leaving him weak-kneed and emotionally ragged outside the Parrish hangar. Mel's Jeep was parked off to the side and the service entrance door was open. He headed in that direction. A commercial jet was powering up to lift off one of the runways so he didn't hear the rumble of a closer threat until it was almost upon him. Turning, he recognized the chromed grill hurtling toward him. He leaped back, trying to get out of its deadly path, but there wasn't time. He was in the air when it clipped him, otherwise he would have shattered upon impact. The hood grazed his hip. Momentum flung him up into the windshield where his head hit hard enough to crack the glass.

He didn't remember hitting the ground, only the incredible agony as he came down on his knee, of finding himself there, sprawled and probably broken beyond repair. Through the blood that nearly blinded him, he saw a blurry outline of the SUV as it skidded to a stop.

And then the bright glare of its backup lights.

It was a long, brutal day, but Mel had no complaints. She was doing what she loved, making a difference when it counted. The exhausting pace kept her too busy to think of anything beyond the next drop of manpower, supplies or water. The mood of camaraderie between her and the men she shuttled was immediate and no one hesitated when it came to placing their trust completely in her hands. And she didn't let them down.

The fire was moving in an erratic path, driven by ever-changing winds and by its own need to consume what it could. Its proximity to Tahoe had a deep terrible fear for Karen seeping beneath her outward control. Just a hop of the ridge would bring hell roaring down upon the beautiful resort town with a cruel indifference. Thinking of her cousin within reach of the beast made her work that much harder, that much smarter. No grandstanding. No risks. Not now.

It was midafternoon when she settled lightly on the tarmac. She meant to take advantage of the break in action while new aerial reconaissance was done to shower and eat and hopefully keep her thoughts from drifting in the wrong direction. Toward the wrong man.

He'd gotten her back in the air. Why? To get her out of the way while he systematically sought the means to crush everything that mattered to her? She stalked toward the hangar, anger masking the less acceptable threads of pain still woven about her heart. Damn Xander Caufield anyway. She wouldn't waste another second of her life pining for…

Then her fierce glare touched on something out of the ordinary. An abandoned shoe in front of the hangar.

A black high-top with laces dangling.

Chapter 11

Alarm struck, sharp and instantaneous.

"Xander?"

As she bent to pick up the shoe, her eye level lowered, bringing her down to where she could see beneath her Jeep. And there, from behind the tire, she saw two feet extended, one in a shoe, one in a sock.

Scrambling, heart pumping, she went to crouch beside the motionless figure stretched out prone upon hot tarmac. She touched a tentative hand to his shoulder and was startled by his abrupt response. He flipped over, using the momentum to lash out, striking upward with the heel of his hand in a hard, defensive move that would have broken her nose, if not her neck, had he managed to connect. She caught his wrists to halt the aggressive if uncoordinated attack, struggling to restrain him. A soft cry escaped her. His face was sticky with blood, his hair matted with it. "Alex? What happened? Are you all right?"

"Mel? Where you at, girl?"

She popped up from behind the Jeep. "Quinn, over here."

The Texan threw off his laid-back attitude at the tone of her voice. By the time he knelt down beside her, it had altered to one of shocked intensity. "Who did this?" he demanded.

She took a breath, fighting to get control of her ragged emotions. "I just got here. I found him like this. You'd better call nine-one-one." Then she gasped again as Xander's hand clamped with surprising strength about her wrist.

"No." Just a whisper but emphatic. His eyes flickered open, rolling and without focus, then slipped shut again.

"Alex, you need a doctor. You need to get to a hospital."

"No. Fine. I'm fine. No hospital. No police."

Police? She hadn't thought that far ahead, but apparently, while he was laid out on the ground seeping vital fluids, Xander had given it ample consideration.

"What happened? Xander, talk to me."

His breathing quickened and his head rolled in agitation. "Didn't see it coming. Hit me. Couldn't get up. So hot. Could I get some water, please?"

"Quinn, help me get him inside."

"Are you sure we should move him?"

"We can't leave him out here. Real easy."

Between them, they toted him in through the hangar and into Mel's rooms in back, laying him down as gently as possible on her unmade bed. By that time, he was out again.

Touching the side of his face, Mel asked, "Do you think we should call someone?"

Quinn was distracted by the way her fingertips moved so tenderly along one blood-smeared cheek. "He said not to. He's got a pretty hard head. Wouldn't want to be the fella that laid him out once he comes around and starts thinking about evens."

"Get me some towels and some warm water."

"Anything else? Maybe a foot massage?"

"Don't be an ass, Quinn."

He brought the requested items then hung back rather sullenly, watching her tend to the injured man.

Once the gore was rinsed away, Mel traced the source back to a split in his scalp just above his ear, the area already swollen and purpling. Not knowing what else to do, she wet a clean towel, folding it into a compress, and set it over the ugly wound. She didn't share Quinn's optimistic view about Xander's well-being. Worry gnawed at her. She would have felt better if he'd returned to consciousness and could tell her more about his circumstances and situation. She wasn't a graceful observer. Inactivity sat restlessly upon her. Then her thoughts caught up a bit and she looked over at Naylor.

"Why were you looking for me?"

"Wanted to let you know I ran into Charley in Tahoe this morning. He and Karen were having breakfast and he wanted me to tell you that he was stopping off to pick up some parts for the chopper. Guess Caufield's check came through for services rendered. Does that mean he'll be moving on?"

Xander had paid her for her time and trouble. How gracious of him. Then her mood quieted. And he'd be leaving. "I don't know what his plans are."

"Much as I'd like to sit here and babysit with you, I got to meet with the helitac foreman. Want me to stop by when I know what our schedule's gonna be for tomorrow?"

"I'll be here."

And he scowled, seeing her attention absorbed by the man in her bed. "Yeah, well, if you need anything, gimme a call on my cell. If he takes a turn for the worse, drag his butt to the E.R., whether he likes it or not."

"I will. Thanks, Quinn."

He didn't think she knew when he left.

He came awake with a jerk. The room was dark. He didn't recognize it. He was lying down. The pain beating through his skull distracted from the lesser agony chewing on his leg.

Where was he? What had happened?

He remembered the lights flashing a vivid warning on the SUV as it came barreling at him in reverse. To finish him off. Somehow, he'd been able to roll and crawl behind Mel's Jeep to become less of a target. Unless his attacker got out and came after him on foot. Then they'd find him no challenge at all. But no one did and then he thought he heard Mel and Quinn, their voices faint and indistinguishable beneath the whine and roar in his head. He remembered hearing something about going to the hospital. No. That would invite questions, would bring in the police who would poke around and get into the business he was trying to wrap up on the q.t. No interference. No outsiders. Nothing to get in his way.

He drifted for a time upon a hot sea of discomfort. What awareness he was able to hang on to like a dangerously inadequate raft in a storm, he couldn't trust. He couldn't think clearly. His vision was as distorted as his thoughts. The strange room took on a living, breathing presence of threat from which there was no escape. Because he couldn't move and he couldn't identify his enemy. Why wasn't he in a hospital? He'd been hit by a car, for God's sake.

He felt a cool touch upon the heat of his forehead. When he moved his head to get out from under it, immense waves of pain swept over him, carrying him out far away from his grasp on consciousness. Then from some shadowy distance, he heard someone say, "Here, take this."

"Wha—?"

Several hard capsules were pushed between his lips. Not knowing what they were, he spit them out with an objecting noise. Then, a firm hand gripped his jaw so he couldn't pull away and the pills were reintroduced along with a rush of water, forcing him to swallow or choke. Released, he panted anxiously, almost feeling the drug entering his system. Helping or harming?

From out of the mists of fever and pain, a soft scent teased him, reminding him of…of someone. It was in the bed linens, on the hand that lightly stroked his cheek.

"Mel?"

"It's all right. I'm taking care of you."

Taking care of him. What did that mean? Until her uncle got back? Or was it Quinn? Or Mel, herself, behind that wheel? It wasn't all right and he wasn't safe. Not here. Not with her.

What had she given him?

They were going to kill him.

Instead of frightening him, that cold certainty brought a sense of purpose to the chaos of his thoughts. He had to get away, away from her and her family. Because they knew he was planning to do them harm.

He lay very still, pretending to sleep while watching through slitted eyes the hazy figure hovering over him. And the moment the figure was gone, he acted quickly, fumbling for the glowing cordless phone at the bedside. It took him four agonizing tries to punch in the right sequence of numbers to bring him the comfort of a familiar voice.

"Help me."

He seemed to be resting and that gave Mel some consolation as she watched over him. She didn't touch him again because that stirred agitation rather than calm. In both of them. When Quinn got back, they were taking him to the hospital.

As she studied the ugly wound marring the perfection of his face, a deep, vengeful fury began to build for whomever had hurt him, for whoever had had the bad sense to nearly bash his head in right on her doorstep. Robbery, she wondered, but a pat of his back pocket revealed the shape of his wallet. What then? She didn't know of anyone he'd irritated to the point of violence. Other than herself.

Unable to resist, she brushed her fingertips over the tops of his where they lay still and tan against her sheets. Remembering with unhappy clarity how they'd felt upon her body, coaxing her to heights of passion. He flicked off her hand with a mutter of complaint then reached down to rub his knee, shifting uncomfortably as he did. Worriedly, she followed suit, and was dismayed to discover the joint swollen within the tight wrap of his jeans. What had he done?

Thinking to ease his distress and to check the extent of his injury, Mel retrieved the butterfly knife she carried when she was out at night alone, flicking open the wicked blade with the intention of slitting the seam. That's when she heard a soft step behind her. Not the arrogant clatter of Quinn's boot heels or Charley's unhurried shuffle, but a light, purposeful pattern of stealth.

She lunged up from the bedside, knife swinging in a deadly arc that stopped just inches from the stranger's throat. The same way his pistol stopped just shy of her forehead. They both froze then he commanded, "Step away from him."

Mel's reply was equally quiet, equally determined. "No."

Their long, tense stalemate was broken by the intrusion of Xander's exasperated demand of, "What the hell are you doing?"

Assuming the remark was for his benefit, the gunman answered, "Saving your ass."

Mel's expression firmed. "That's what I thought I was doing."

Xander muttered a groggy oath and scrubbed his hand over his face. Wincing. "Back down the both of you. Kyle, Mel Parrish. Kyle, what are you doing here?"

Holstering his pistol with reluctance, D'Angelo regarded his friend peevishly. "Pardon me for taking your ranting phone call seriously. Something about you being hit by a car and about to be killed, if I recall correctly."

"Hit by a car?" Mel stared down at him, aghast.

"I don't remember..." But the phone was under the covers, the line still open so Kyle could trace it and come running to his rescue. From Mel? His gaze flickered up, startled then wary. He couldn't meet her questioning look. "Sorry. I was kind of out of it for a while there."

Kyle brushed by Mel to kneel down at his friend's side. Expression somber, he anchored Xander's head between his hands, checking his eyes for equal dilation and then the nasty wound. "You all right?"

"You mean other than being hit by a car?"

"Did you get a plate number?"

"Sorry, no. But I can identify the tire treads that were about to run over my face."

"Don't cop an attitude with me." His gruff voice was offset by his extreme gentleness. "Banged up anywhere else?"

"I was just about to check his knee," Mel began. "It's all swollen." Hit by a car. Her mind reeled, thinking shattered bones, internal bleeding, punctured organs. And here she was trying to treat him with a couple of ibuprofen. She caught a glimpse of the high top sitting on her nightstand.

He'd been knocked right out of his shoe.

A terrible shaking started in her belly.

"Let's have a look." He dismissed Xander's sound of protest impatiently. "It's not like either of us hasn't seen your dumb butt before." Then his gaze slashed warily toward Mel as he peeled down the snug denims. Xander's harsh inhale brought his attention back and his expression worked for a silent minute before he muttered a tight, "Ah, jeez, Alex. Look at you."

And Mel looked, feeling sick inside.

His hip was mottled by ugly bruising. His knee had ballooned like a seedless watermelon. And his temper was strained as he snapped, "What part of hit by a car didn't you understand? Give me back the dignity of my pants and get me to the hospital."

Wrestling them back up was worse then taking them down. He was panting and sweating, eyes squeezed shut by the time Kyle allowed him any sympathy.

"Anything mashed up inside that I need to know about before I move you? Can't have you going hemorrhagic in my rental car."

"Your concern is touching."

"Come on. Let's get you up and out of here."

Mel spoke up suddenly. "I'm going with you."

Both men looked at her, Xander with surprise, Kyle with more subtle emotions. He was the one to reply coolly. "No need for that. I've got him."

Xander said nothing.

So, he was going to just hobble out of her life? Once he left, there would be no reason for his return. She couldn't just let him go. Not like this. "I'm coming, too," she restated, meeting Xander's impassive stare. "I owe you one."

He looked slightly uncomfortable of the reminder to the ambulance ride he'd taken with her, but relented. "All right." He glanced at the phone in his hand and quickly punched in a list of commands.

"Making reservations at the E.R.?"

He smiled up at her, the gesture narrow and somehow sad. "No. I was just— Nothing. It's not important." He dropped the receiver onto the nightstand and held his arm up, waiting for Kyle to dip under it to hoist him to his feet. Or rather, one foot. He sagged against his friend, good knee buckling.

"Come on, Xander. Is that all you got? I seem to recall walking to the ambulance with three broken ribs, a cracked collarbone and my arm fractured in two places."

"You didn't do it alone. Gimme a break, Angie." But he was sucking deep breaths and drawing himself upright to meet the challenge until they were eye to steady eye. Kyle smiled faintly.

"Ready?"

Mel slipped in under his other arm, providing just enough balance for him to make his way between them. He dragged himself across the back seat, where he could stretch out his leg and lean against the door with eyes closed. He didn't look good. Mel got up front with their prickly driver. He kept his eyes on the road with the occasional glance into the rearview to see how Xander was faring. She might as well have not existed.

He was a good-looking man, features pleasingly handsome with a laid-back confidence she couldn't imagine from Xander. Warm brown eyes, mile-wide smile complete with dimples, dark hair buzzed short, and a buff build that could have put him on a hot and sweaty cover of *Men's Fitness* rather than Xander's coolly elegant *GQ* flair. She couldn't picture them as friends, as having anything in common. And then she remembered what Kyle had called him. They'd known each other when Xander was still Alex. And that explained everything.

Then Kyle glanced her way. He would have pulled the trigger without blinking an eye if he'd determined she was a threat. His quick glare said the jury was still out on that decision. Which didn't make the ride any more comfortable for her.

Xander was wisked away in a wheelchair, leaving the two of them standing awkwardly in the waiting room.

"You don't have to stay," Kyle told her bluntly.

She could be just as rude. "Neither do you."

"You don't know anything about him."

"No, I don't," she agreed softly. "But that doesn't mean I don't want to."

"He's not an easy guy to get to know."

"I'm patient."

"He won't give you the time."

The bluntly spoken truth caught her right between the eyes. "You might be wrong," she challenged with enough menace to make him regard her narrowly.

He gazed at her for a long, contemplative moment then shook his head. "No. I'm not wrong."

His calm certainty shook her more than she wanted to admit. She responded to the fear with a defiant bravado. "You might know him, but you don't know me."

"Oh, yeah, I do, lady. I know you. You're nothing he needs. You don't have what it takes."

The factual way he stated that, without malice, without any particular unpleasantness, made her wonder if he wasn't right. But still she asked, "What does it take?"

"When we were dumb kids, eighteen, just out of school, we went climbing. Somehow, my carabiner came loose. I fell a good thirty feet, bouncing a couple of times off a rock wall before Alex was able to clip on. He held on to me, dangling five hundred feet up until he could swing me over to a tiny little ledge. I was all busted up, couldn't climb, and he couldn't lower me down. Some of the most hellacious weather I've ever seen blew up. Sleet, cold, dark. He could have climbed out of there, left me and gone for help. It would have been the smart thing to do. It's what he should have done. It's what I asked him to do. Begged him to do. But he wouldn't leave me there unprotected when there was a chance that I wouldn't make it. It was twelve hours before a rescue party came for us. It never occurred to him that he didn't have to stay there and risk freezing to death with me. Who the hell would do that for him?"

"I suspect you would." She paused, adding, "So would I."

That plainly shook him. Then he threw off the gloves. "So why did he call me to protect him from you?"

While she stared at him blankly, horrified by his suggestion, he turned and walked away from her.

Manipulating the pair of crutches, Xander swung through into the waiting room and paused there for a long minute considering the scene. Kyle sat on one side of the room watching sports scores scroll beneath an inaudible commentator. His features were grim as granite. Mel stood as far away from him as possible, staring out into the parking lot. Her posture was ramrod stiff. Obviously, they hadn't struck up any fond connection. So, who to approach?

"Hey, tough guy. Knew they couldn't keep you down."

Xander never thought he'd be so grateful to see Quinn Naylor. His booming voice garnered the attention of both sulking parties and brought them to him, Kyle in a hurry, Mel more slowly, more cautiously.

"What did they say?"

Xander looked at his friend as if he was a dolt. "That I was hit by a car. Let's get out of here before they decide they want to give you a CT scan in search of intelligent life."

Quinn's laugh drew scowling looks from the staff at the desk but the other two never cracked a smile.

"I'm supposed to give a statement to the police. Let's get out of here. I need to sit down and pass out."

Kyle shot a warning volley to Mel and growled, so there would be no question, "I'll bring the car around."

Too tired to try to navigate the complexities, Xander simply nodded. Once Kyle was gone, he glanced at Quinn. "What are you doing here, cowboy? Taking bets on which one of my vital organs they'd need to remove?"

"I had spleen, seeing as how you have more than enough of that already." He grinned. "Mel called for a ride."

He gave Mel a curious look and her answer was a riddle.

"It seems there wasn't enough room on the ledge for all three of us."

"What?"

"I just wanted to stay long enough to make sure you were all right. I see you are. Good night."

"Mel, wait."

She paused, her head bowing for an instant then the starch was back in her spine. "Quinn, would you mind getting the truck?"

"What? You can't walk now, either?" Then he looked between them and mumbled sourly, "Yeah, right. Get the truck."

When it was just the two of them, Mel turned. It took a long time for her gaze to lift to met his. And then it was with double-barreled velocity.

"So, how was I going to do it?"

"Do what?"

His confusion only pumped up the action. "Obviously my attempt to run you down failed, so was I resorting to poison? You spit those pain relievers out fast enough. Was I going to hold you captive in my bed until you starved to death or just get sick of you altogether and smother you?"

"Mel—"

"How could you think such a thing? How could you think—"

"Mel, I was out of my head."

"Oh, no. Never that. Your mind is always working at one-hundred percent. Why else would you be on the way to emergency and have the sense to erase your no-last-name friend's number off my phone?" Tears sparked in her eyes. She was too angry to brush them away.

He didn't attempt to deny anything. Instead, he asked, "Who did you tell about who I was? Who knows besides your cousin?"

"I didn't tell anyone." She couldn't bear the thought of anyone else knowing what a fool she'd been. Then her thoughts quickened. "Why?"

"Where's your uncle, Mel?"

"Why?" she demanded again, her bluster not quite concealing the alarm in her eyes.

"Someone tried to run me off the road on my way back from Tahoe this morning. That same someone was waiting outside your hangar to finish the job." He let that sink in for a moment then asked again, "Mel, where was your uncle today?"

"I don't know."

She was lying.

He started to maneuver past her. She caught his arm, nearly costing him his balance. Her gaze held a fierce intensity.

"How could you think I would ever let any harm come to you?" She reached up to take his face between her palms, pulling him down for a hard, lip-bruising kiss. "I wouldn't have left you on that ledge, Alex. Not for a second."

Then she pushed away quickly and fled for the parking lot. When he tried to spin about, his feet tangled around the tips of his crutches, delaying him long enough for her to jump into Quinn's four-by-four without a backward glance. He was still hopping for a center of gravity when Kyle returned to brace him up.

"What's wrong?"

Xander sighed in frustration. "She kept saying something about not leaving me on some ledge. What's that about?"

Kyle shrugged. "No idea. Come on. Let's get your stuff."

As he helped Xander get into the rental, Kyle D'Angelo looked after the rapidly disappearing pickup truck, his expression closed down tight.

Yes, she would. In a pair of seconds.

Chapter 12

The bed was made up in his room, the corners tight, the spread smooth. As if he and Mel had never tangled up in them only twenty-four hours ago. As if nothing had ever happened. He stood in the doorway, leaning heavily on the crutches, heart hanging even heavier, still.

Kyle brushed past him and strode directly to the closet, pulling out his meager luggage with an eagerness to be gone. He tossed Xander's garment bag on the foot of the bed and began to load the contents of the dresser into it.

"I'll save you out a set of clothes so you can change before we leave. You want to grab a shower first?"

Xander couldn't focus on anything beyond that suitcase filling with the evidence of his nomadic life. "I'd probably just go down the drain."

Kyle gave him a glance. "Sit down before you fall down."

He should have taken the chair, but the bed looked so much more inviting. Once he'd eased down onto the edge of it, it was a short boneless spill to the pillows. He fished into his coat pocket finally locating his prescription, letting it flutter to the bedspread. "I'm supposed to get this filled."

Kyle glanced at the script and raised his brows. "Ooh, nice. You won't be feeling pain anytime soon."

Xander could have argued that. The numbness seeping through his system only emphasized the empty ache in his soul. That soul Mel told him he didn't have. Perhaps she was right. "I never got the money trans-ferred over. Have to do that first thing…tomorrow." Because it was too difficult to hold his eyes open, he let them close. Shutting out the sight of Kyle removing all traces that he'd ever been in Reno, Nevada. And his sense of melancholy kept swelling. "I thought I was going to die, Angie."

The sounds of industry ceased for a long moment then resumed hurriedly.

"It's the first time I've been scared of anything since I was a kid," he continued, his words beginning to slur together slightly. "Except living. That make any kind of sense?"

"No. It's just the drugs."

Xander let his head roll, negating Kyle's gruff conclusion. "In my whole life, I haven't done anything worthwhile. I haven't cared if I made a damn bit of difference to anyone."

"Well, thanks for that, Alex. You sure know how to sell a friendship off cheap."

Because he sounded genuinely angry, Xander struggled

to explain. "You've got lots of friends, Kyle. You've got close family. Everyone likes you."

"Yeah, I know lots of people and we have a lot of laughs. And so would you if you'd just lighten up. But when it comes right down to it, when it matters, really matters, how many of my good friends do you think would stand by me and…"

"And what?"

"Nothing. Forget it."

Xander slit his eyes open. Kyle D'Angelo was a blur but Xander's mind was suddenly crystal clear. "What? Go out on a ledge for you? So that's what she meant."

Kyle didn't answer.

"Do you know what scared me, Kyle?"

"What?"

"Knowing I'd never see her again. How crazy is that?"

"Pretty damn crazy. Shut up and get some sleep. You'll be your old cynical self in the morning and we'll get back to business as usual."

"I don't want to be back to business as usual."

"And what do you want? A nice little suburban nine-to-five with the woman of your dreams?"

"Yeah. I think I do."

"Well, get over it, Alex, because it doesn't exist. You'd get bored and hate it and she'd get angry and hate you. There is no happily-ever-after."

Xander was silent, giving his thoughts time to assemble before saying, softly, with all the meaning in the world, "I'm sorry, Kyle. I haven't been any kind of friend to you. It's all been about me."

"Alex, you don't need to—"

"Yes, I do. When this is done, I'll help you find her."

Dead silence then an explosive, "What? What the hell are you talking about?"

"We'll find her and then we'll both forget about being so miserable. How's that sound?"

"It sounds crazy." It sounded terrifying. "And you can forget about it. Alex, you— Alex?"

He was out cold. Leaving Kyle D'Angelo in a panic of sudden possibilities.

He'd checked out of the hotel.

Mel tried to concentrate on flying with that fact gnawing on the edge of her thoughts. She'd planned to let it go, to let him go, but she just couldn't go up without knowing. So she'd called. Alexander Caufield had turned in his room key at seven-thirty that morning. And she had no idea where he'd disappeared to.

As it was, she had to look no farther than her front door.

He was leaning against the bumper of her Jeep, his crutches resting next to him. No designer suit, no metal briefcase, no perfect grooming. Just rumpled hair, dark glasses, sweat jacket and baggy shorts above his heavily bandaged knee. And bare feet. A single black high-top sat on the hood of her vehicle. The other one was still on her bedside table.

"Hey," he called out tentatively. "How are things up there?"

"Could be better, could be worse. You?"

"Could be better, could be worse." A faint smile. Not quite an invitation. So she extended one.

"Come on in out of the sun. I'll stand you to a diet cola."

She walked by him, not offering to help, because she wasn't sure she could trust herself to get that up close and personal. She heard the clatter of his crutches but made herself keep walking.

"You've got my other shoe," he told her.

"A man of your means must own more than one pair."

"They're the only pair I like."

"So you came to tie up loose ends, so to speak?"

"Yes."

He'd come to say goodbye. Or to ask more probative questions about her involvement in his case. Either option left her less than enthusiastic. He glanced around the quiet hangar.

"Where's Charley?"

"Haven't seen him since he gassed me up this morning. Probably out creating criminal mayhem someplace. I'll be sure to pass the details on to you as they become available."

"Stop it, Mel." He sounded weary and frustrated and she didn't want to care.

"Stop what? You started it, after all." She turned to confront him just as he was peeling down his sunglasses. She winced at the sight of his spectacular shiner. "Ouch."

"Could we not do this, Mel?"

"Why, Xander, we're not going to be doing anything." She left him standing in the hangar and returned from her room, thrusting the second sneaker at him. "Was there anything else?"

"Did you mean what you said about the ledge?"

He looked as surprised as she was at the way he blurted that out, but he didn't try to back out of it. So she answered simply.

"Yes."

"I want a second night with you, Mel."

That was the last thing she expected to hear from him. Because her pulse was suddenly hopscotching, she drawled, "I'm afraid I'm all booked up for the season."

A narrow smile twitched upon his lips. "Then I guess I'll just have to wait here in case you have a cancellation."

A purely sinful amount of anticipation swirled around the panic. "You'll have a long, long wait."

"I've got nothing else more important that needs doing."

"No families to ruin, no innocent females to seduce?"

"Not even any not-so-innocent ones."

"I wouldn't want to compromise your high moral standards."

His grin broke wide and dazzling. "Accusing me of having morals now, are you? That's low. You've made better arguments."

She sighed in aggravation. "It's probably because I really don't want to argue at all."

His mood instantly quieted. His eyes smoldered. "What do you want to do?"

What the hell.

"I want to go for two."

He drew a long, shaky breath. "All right. Good answer."

"But considering you can't even stand up…"

"What I had in mind didn't require me standing up. But if I lie down, I'll probably be unconscious in five seconds and I plan on taking a little longer than that. Sitting is good. I can sit just fine."

She thought quickly, a bit frantically, discarding the dining room set with its wobbly wooden legs, her backless office chair, the saggy sofa and love seat that sat out in plain view in the hangar. "Are you sure you're up for this? I mean with all the pain meds and—"

With his palm at the small of her back, he pulled her up flush against his very impressive response. "I'm up for anything. As long as it doesn't involve stair climbing. Or cars. I'm really not into cars at the moment."

"Follow me."

He thumped behind her as she led the way to the hulking Shorts C-23A Sherpa personnel jump carrier Charley was restoring as funds were available. Work had been at a standstill for a long while. Ducking under the struts between high wing and bulky body and the large blade of the turboprop, she opened the port-side door and nodded inside. "Watch that first step, then after that, it's smooth sailing."

Using the crutches for balance, he took a step up on his good leg. Then, hanging onto the door frame, he gave his crutches a toss inside, eased down on his rump and scooted back inside. Then, it was just a matter of dragging himself up onto one of the seats while Mel closed the door and pushed the lap belts aside.

"Good afternoon, ladies and gentlemen. I'm Melody and I'll be your flight attendant this evening. Please put your seats back. If things get bumpy or should you require any oxygen during our flight, I'd be happy to assist you in any way to make your trip more comfortable." She dropped his seat back at a forty-five-degree angle and climbed up to straddle his thighs.

"I'm Alex. Fly me."

"Be patient, sir. According to FAA regulations, I have to instruct you on the proper insertion of your lap belt."

He gripped her by the taut seat of her denims. "Tab A into Slot B and tighten. Got it."

She put a palm to either side of his face, her thumb tracing the colorful circle beneath his eye. She felt it only fair to warn him. "This is going to complicate things."

"I don't care."

"You will."

"I'll worry about it then." His fingertips caressed her cheek. The bandages were off his hands. His touch was achingly gentle. "You are so beautiful."

She gave a snort of disbelief. "I am not. I'm all dirty and smoky and I don't have any makeup on."

"Beautiful," he repeated, and the soft, dark glow in his eyes reflected that truth. All the barriers were down in his expression. Probably the drugs. His relaxed smile exuded an approachable and honest warmth. She couldn't resist taking advantage of that agreeably yielding mouth.

He was still smiling when she lifted up from their kiss.

"What?" she asked, following the sensuous shape of his lips with her forefinger.

"I don't know. Just really happy to be here with you." He sounded slightly amazed, and she understood that he wasn't accustomed to that particular emotion. It should have scared her to be the focus of his tender feelings. That it didn't, should have alarmed her even more. "I want to spend more time with you."

That brought a note of reality to her mood. "Your friend told me I didn't have it."

"Kyle? What else did he tell you, my good and soon to be severely bruised friend?"

"That you were hard to get to know."

His fingers were playing in her hair, twining, combing, scrunching. "I'm feeling extremely zen at the moment. What do you want to know?"

Resting forearms on his shoulders, she picked the question he'd be most likely to resist.

"Tell me about your father."

He didn't even blink. "I don't know anything about him, only that my mother came home after spring break to announce that she was dropping out of college and having a baby. Knowing my mom's taste in men, he probably wouldn't have stuck around anyway. We didn't need him. It wasn't like we were on welfare. And I had plenty of 'uncles' to emulate while growing up."

"Did any of them take an interest in you?"

His laugh was short and self-deprecating. "Yeah, that's just what they were interested in, playing father figure to a nerdy kid who had no talent for anything except getting in the way of them having a good time with my mother."

"That's what your mom thought you were? In the way?"

He laughed off her tender concern. "She loved the hell out of me. She just didn't know how to be a mother. I was Alexander Caufield III. Mom named me that just to piss off her old man, but he kind of liked it, having a namesake, an heir to the throne. Except that I didn't have a creative bone in my body. So much for minding the music empire. I liked tangible, solid things. Reliable things, like numbers, facts. I could memorize anything. My grandfather used to say everyone had the skills to succeed. Failing to find that skill and hone it to perfection was unacceptable. He couldn't tolerate a user or a loser, which was why he never liked any of my mother's boyfriends. Am I mistaken or was there supposed to be some good sweaty sex involved here somewhere between the two of us?"

She unzipped his hooded jacket. There was nothing but smooth skin over hard muscle beneath it. A tempting distraction but not enough to discourage her from learning more. She appreciated the feel of his precision-cut pecs while asking, "So when did this metamorphosis take place, from Alexander to Alex?"

"After surviving puberty, I put on sixty pounds and seven inches, got rid of my acne and my braces, got contact lenses and worked out until I could bench-press a small foreign car. Along with half the cheerleading squad. I was insufferably obnoxious."

"Worse than now?"

Her lips rode the vibration of his chuckle. "Hard to believe, I know. I had money, looks, toys, backstage passes to the hottest venues in town. All the groupie chicks wanted to boff me, all the popular guys wanted me to hook them up."

"Former-nerd nirvana." She imagined what a ferocious heartbreaker he must have been back then.

"Big time," he admitted with some chagrin. He was kneading the back of her neck, his touch light, his mood pensive. "I was out of control. A wild boy. Then new husband number three or four came along. He was a straight arrow, a developer. I don't know how he and my mom got together. Evan Sanders. After three months, he'd had enough of me skipping classes, sleeping in until three, leaving wrecked convertibles and girlfriends lying on the front lawn with their tops down and he packed my snotty butt off to the same prep school he'd attended. He wasn't my father and I hated him for caring about what happened to me."

She straightened, soothing the frown lines from the corners of his eyes, kissing him softly, with just enough teasing tongue action to coax back his smile.

"So how was prep school?" she goaded. "A bunch of rich, good-looking spoiled brats? You must have fit right in."

"No. Not at all. I looked at them and saw everything despicable that I'd become. That was my wake-up call, that and an awesome left jab from Kyle D'Angelo. His date threw up on the leather seats of my brand-new Italian sports car. I got loud about it and Kyle laid me out cold. While I was getting my tooth capped, he was having my upholstery cleaned."

"And fast friends ever since." She smiled somewhat wryly.

"Yes, we were. He was heading toward prelaw and criminal justice because of his attorney father, and since that sounded a lot more interesting than being an accountant for a bunch of overindulgent rock stars, I started thinking about investment and business law. That's where I found what I was really good at."

She folded her arms atop his chest, leaning there, watching the quiet lines of his face strengthen, the mellow heat in his eyes chill over in a familiar glaze. "What were you good at?"

"Being in control. I didn't want to count someone else's money, I wanted to manipulate it, court it, seduce it, use it and get rid of it when it stopped performing."

"Quit," she drawled. "You're turning me on."

He grinned. "It was a turn-on. I loved everything about it. The research details, the stability of numbers, the variables of the market. Competitive, exciting, power suits, power lunches, power trips."

"Better than sex."

His hand slipped up under her T-shirt to snap open the front of her cotton bra with an impressive expertise. "I'm still just a geek in a designer label."

"Yeah, but you wear it so well. Smart, powerful men are sexy." She stripped off her shirt and let it drop to the carpet. He sat for a moment, staring fixedly at the open clasp.

"And we're also cold and self-absorbed and have a scary gift of…blankness."

"And you started calling yourself Xander."

He didn't say anything more for a while as he pushed away the soft cling of cotton to lay her breasts bare. His touch was whisper soft as it circumvented both generous globes. The attentive claim of his mouth, wet and warm on first one then the other pebbled tip, distracted her from conversation for several bliss-filled minutes. Finally, when his head was resting heavy against her and his breath stroked in short, quick bursts along her bare skin, Mel risked everything to ask, "Alex, what did you do that was so terrible you're still punishing yourself for it?"

He froze, not even breathing. Then slowly he eased back into his seat, head bowed, expression shadowed.

"Alex?"

His gaze flashed up, the dark depths swimming in grief and guilt before flickering away again.

"I was successful. I made an unholy amount of money for my grandfather and Mom and for myself. Alexander the First wanted me to work for him exclusively, but I was arrogant and full of myself and didn't want to be on anyone's leash. He didn't like that much. But Evan did. He was proud of me and said so. He tried to talk to me about business responsibility and ethics and priorities, but being a punk, I blew him off. He and my mom were going through a rough patch. She'd started developing some new talent, some Brooklyn kid younger than me who looked great in music videos and apparently skinny-dipping in our pool. If she'd been smart… But she wasn't and she still isn't and I was in the process of losing father number three or four and angry as hell about it. Because even though we didn't see eye to eye, I liked the way Evan took care of my mom.

"He was finishing up a big development property in Colorado. He had every cent he owned and could borrow sunk into it. When my mom put a freeze on their accounts, he came to me and asked if I'd front him a loan just to tide him over. He was in the process of bringing on a partner and it was short-term, just until he could get some working capital in hand. I laughed at him, Mel. I told him he was a bad risk, just like I'd been a bad risk when he shipped me off to boarding school to get rid of me. I crushed his dream because he'd hurt my feelings." He looked up at her, his eyes glittery.

"He went to prison, Mel. He's serving fifteen to thirty for conspiracy to commit arson, fraud and manslaughter. And I put him there."

Chapter 13

For a moment, his summation shocked her into silence. Then she demanded, practically, defensively, "How was what happened to him your fault? You're not responsible for anything that he did."

His compressed smile nearly broke her heart. "Don't try making excuses for me being a bastard."

"You are, and I'm not."

"Thanks for being so blunt."

She shrugged it off. "You refused a loan. That's business."

"No." He shook his head slowly. "It was personal and it was family. I should have...listened. I should have realized how desperate he was. I had the money. But I was—"

"What?"

He struggled for the answer, trying to come up with

some simple way to express all the complexities of emotion he hadn't understood then and hated to recognize now. Evan Sanders had offered him his one chance to know what it would be like to have a real family. Not the dysfunctional chaos that usually surrounded his mother, but a grounded, rational adult who could offer stability, advice and, more importantly, permanence. Sanders made their big rambling palace a home, had his mother behaving like a grown-up capable of having conversations. Sanders called him son, made him believe he'd become a reliable fixture in his future.

She touched his cheek with a gentle understanding. "You loved him and he let you down."

"I let him down, Mel. If I'd lent him the money, he could have finished the project and paid off his creditors. Instead, I let him sink into a debt he couldn't get out of. The man he took on as a partner was useless. He'd only stepped in because he thought our family fortune would bail them out. When it didn't, he found another way to make a profit. It was a dry summer. There were fires popping up all over and one of them just happened to consume the project and the partner. The investigators found evidence of arson and Evan was arrested.

"My family abandoned him. Bad press, you know. I never visited him. I never wrote. I believed the verdict. Until Kyle brought me a handful of clippings about similar fire losses. He liked Evan and never believed for a second that he was involved in anything illegal. He'd been doing a freelance job for an insurance company and heard the scuttlebutt about some fire bug cashing in on their policies. They wouldn't give me any information when I asked directly so I decided to find out on my own. I walked away from my investments and Kyle got me set up working insurance-fraud cases. I found something else I was good at. It's all numbers and probabilities. And while I was working those little cases, I was gathering what little information I could on those possible arsons."

Because the chilling gleam was back in his eyes, she found it more comfortable to lean against him, her head on his shoulder, her arms tight about his middle. "And what did you find out?" she asked at last, knowing but not wanting to hear.

"That the same variables kept coming up. Numbers are honest, Mel. They can't lie. And they placed your family on the front steps of every case. And within a few months of a policy payoff, a big chunk of your family debts would disappear."

Her eyes squeezed shut. Her protest was tight throated. "It could be a coincidence."

His arms came up slowly, curling about her as if his embrace could protect her from his next words. "I can't prove that it's not. Not yet, anyway."

Alarm spiked through her. "But soon. That's what you and Kyle are up to. Something's going on right now, isn't it?"

"I can't talk to you about this. And I can't walk away."

"It's my family, my friends. What am I supposed to do, Alex? Help you put them in prison?"

She felt his lips move upon her hair. His voice was a low, hoarse rumble. "No. Of course not. You love them. I'd expect you to protect them any way you can."

She pulled back, out of his arms, to command his somber gaze. "How did you expect me to protect them? By running you over with a car?"

"I hope not." His smile was woefully unconvincing.

"But someone did. Someone tried to kill you because you've gotten too close. And I can't—I won't—believe it was Charley or Quinn or any of the men I've been ferrying into hell all these years. I can't believe it, Alex."

"I don't want to believe it, either. I like them. All of them. I've liked being a part of what they are and what they do. So what am I supposed to do?"

She linked her hands behind his head and leaned toward him until their foreheads met and their eyes closed. "You stay safe. When I saw your shoe…" The words choked off thickly. And she kissed him, on the cheek, on the colorful crescent under his eye, lightly where he had twelve stitches, then softly on the lips, lingering there, savoring the sweetness she would have missed for the rest of her days, until just the taste of him could no longer satisfy the enormity of what she was feeling. "We won't talk about this anymore. Not when we're together. You won't ask me questions I can't answer and I won't ask you not to do what I know you have to do. Deal?"

"It's not going to be easy, Mel," was his soft warning, whispered against her mouth.

"I can handle it, as long as I get to handle you."

"Fair enough."

"An when this is done—"

"When this is done."

"I'm no groupie chick but I really want you, Alex Caufield."

"About time we got to the sex part."

"Not just sex. It's way more involved than that, I'm afraid."

"And that scares you, does it?"

"Right down to the underwear I'm not wearing. How about you?"

"Absolutely terrified." But there was no hesitation in the way he drew her to him for an openmouthed, tongue-thrusting kiss that involved them completely to the limit of their shared breath. Then she was undoing his shorts, standing briefly to peel down her own cargo pants while his hot gaze tracked their descent. He was fumbling with his wallet.

"My mom insisted that I always wear my rubbers when there was the chance it was going to get wet."

"We wouldn't want you to catch cold."

As she settled back on his lap, she bumped his knee. The sharp shock of pain made him gasp. And then stare in dismay at the square of foil that disappeared down the tiny crack between the seats. Cursing, he tried to go after it, unable to wedge his hand into the unyielding space. And then Mel slid down over him, a hot tight glove of flesh over flesh, blanking his mind to everything but that exquisite fit. She lifted and lowered to seal the deal.

"We're not going to catch anything, are we?" she murmured against his lips.

"What? No, of course not." His hands cupped her firm bottom, adjusting the rhythm. Then all he had to do was lean back and enjoy the trip all the way to its rough but satisfying landing. Ridiculously content, he let his eyes close, drifting on a wonderful lethargy until he felt Mel's light kiss.

"How did you get here, Alex?"

He smiled, lazily. "I had a great flight."

"Here to the hangar," she clarified.

"Cab."

"Stay the night." Because a hint of vulnerable uncertainty crept into her tone, he opened his eyes. She was well kissed, tousled and naked. What did she expect him to say?

"I'm not going to be good for much more than sleep."

"Sleep with me."

"I need a shower."

"Shower with me."

"I need clean clothes. And if you say you'll do my laundry, I'll marry you."

He'd said it in fun, but the complete silence that followed stretched out uncomfortably until Mel knocked her knuckles beneath his chin and smiled thinly. "I don't do laundry."

And wisely, he didn't reply. Saying the *M* word out loud in any context spooked him and he watched her cautiously as she eased off his lap and backed out of the awkward situation. She slipped her shirt on, then playfully lassoed him around the neck with her bra.

"Will you let me take advantage of you?"

"In the bed or in the shower?"

"Both."

He groaned. "Take all you like. I'm just not sure I have anything left to give."

He was wrong on both counts.

He wasn't sure what woke him. He'd fallen asleep so deep and dreamlessly, he'd thought it would take a nuclear attack to rouse him. He could hear the thump of their clothes tumbling intimately entwined through the fluff dry.

The vibration quickened a dull ache in his head. Movement sent pain ripping through his knee. His pain meds had worn off with a fierce vengeance. Stifling a moan of complaint, he lay still, trying to will himself back to sleep to no avail.

"Mel, where are my pills?" he muttered groggily. "I'll let you drug me and have your way with me again."

No answer.

Then he realized the other thing that had woken him. The deliciously soft heat of her body spooned up behind his was missing. He reached back to find the sheet warm but empty.

"Melody?"

Mumbling a soft curse, he dragged himself upright and snagged his crutches. If he could find the washer and dryer, he was sure to find the bottle of medication he'd been carrying in his pocket. Even though she claimed laundry wasn't her thing, surely she'd check the pockets first.

He stumped halfway across the room then he heard voices from out in the hangar. One was Mel's. The other a man's. For a moment, he considered inviting himself into the conversation, but the fact that he had not so much as a sock to put on gave him some degree of hesitation. Then he recognized Charley Parrish's voice, only the cadence was odd, the syllables slurred. He was roaring drunk. And Mel was scolding him like a wayward teenager.

"What are you thinking? Driving in this condition? I thought your car was in the shop?"

"I had a rental. I had to take it back and I got to talking old times with Sid, you remember Sid Petroni. Him and Marcy, Paddy and your mom, and me and your Aunt Terri used to go out on the town together. Those were good days. Good days."

"I remember Sid. He always kept black licorice behind the counter and he taught me how to use a pneumatic air gun so I wouldn't tell Mom you were playing poker for money."

"Yeah. And then you started cleaning our pockets out regularly."

Xander grinned at that, leaning on his crutches to listen. He could imagine a tough little tomboy flipping cards and raking in chips. A sudden poignant twist of emotions took him by surprise, startling him into an immediate panic that quieted just as soon as he recognized the feeling. Something so new and strong he had to keep reminding himself what it was.

"God, I love you, Melody Parrish."

Saying it out loud, even as a whisper to himself, made the truth easier to embrace.

"You and Karen mean everything to me. You know that, Mellie."

"I know, Charley."

"I wouldn't hurt you for the world. Not for the world."

"I know."

"No, you don't know. You don't know. You don't know how sorry I was about your mom."

Silence. Then a more strained, "I know."

"How could you? You were just a little girl. Paddy's little girl."

"Charley, you need to go home before you fall down. Let me call you a cab. Or I'll drive you."

"It was my fault, Mel."

"I know. You never mean to have one more for the road."

"Your mom was my fault. She was such a special woman and he treated her, and you, so badly."

"What are you talking about, Charley?"

"June. She could never see the weakness in him. She always wanted to believe everything he told her. That he was sorry. That things would get better. He was a liar, Mel. He never meant any of it for more than a day or two. I spent my whole life apologizing for him. Covering up his mistakes."

"I don't want to hear any more of this tonight." Her tone was sharp with irritation. And fear. Xander could hear the pull of anxiety undercutting her fierce words. "Sit over here on the couch while I call you a taxi."

"It was my fault, Mellie. I didn't mean for it to happen. I didn't mean for any of it to happen. I've been trying to make it right. All these years, I've been trying to make it right for you and Karen. And Paddy, too. He didn't deserve it. Not like that. He was my brother. My brother."

"Sit down, Charley. Come on. Get your shoes off."

"For you girls. I did it for you girls. Say you forgive me, Mel. Say you forgive me." He broke into great drunken sobs that, with Mel's quiet comforting, dwindled down to mournful hiccups. But her gentle assurances didn't comfort Xander.

What the hell was Charley Parrish confessing to?

It was two-thirty by the time she got her uncle tucked in and was able to shuffle back to bed. In less than two hours, she'd be getting up again. It almost wasn't worth the effort to take off her clothes. Until she stood at the edge of the mattress, looking down at the figure stretched out beneath her sheets.

Alex Caufield. He was so beautiful in repose, with the lines of his face relaxed, with the cares of the moment forgotten. He was everything she'd ever wanted. Gorgeous, sharp, challenging, maddening, unexpectedly fun, an extraordinary lover who surprised her like the complexity of a really good, really expensive wine. Sweet, yet a bit dry at first sip then developing into a rich, boldly satisfying depth when savored. She wanted nothing more than to roll the taste of him about her palate...forever.

Except for the fact that he was about to crush her, destroying everything she'd ever loved, everything she had left. And then he was going to leave her.

She eased down onto the bed beside him, fully dressed, lying on her back to deny herself the comfort of cuddling close to him. He was right. She was scared. Scared of caring for him, believing in him, loving him. Because she knew it was going to end badly, with him breaking her spirit whether he meant to or not. When he'd jokingly mentioned marriage, all her hopes and dreams had seized up around her heart, squeezing with a bittersweet intensity. But of course he wasn't serious, would never be serious about someone like her. What could she offer when he'd admittedly already sampled half the women in the free world and found them wanting. His money and his background didn't matter to her. They were more of a hindrance than an attractant. But they were part of who he was. And Alexander III wouldn't show up at his grandfather's mansion with a decidedly unsophisticated grease monkey fly girl on his arm no matter what his hot, lambent gaze might insinuate.

And as much as she wanted to roll up tight against him and hang on for dear life, she was going to have to let him go. And knowing it was killing her. Because, as Kyle D'Angelo said, she wasn't what he needed.

"Hey," he murmured softly, his palm running up and down her arm. If he was wondering why she was dressed, he didn't say so. "Everything all right?"

"Sure. Fine."

He caught up her hand in the curl of his own, lifting it first to his mouth so he could brush his lips across her knuckles, then holding it over his heart so she could feel its steady beat beneath her palm. "What can I do for you, Mel? Name it. Anything at all."

Pay off my debts so I don't have to panic every time the mail comes. Take me away from here so I don't have to worry and work so hard all the time. So I won't be so alone. Promise me you'll love me forever and won't ever, ever hurt me or my family. Just go away, far away so I can pretend no one as wonderful and perfect as you ever existed.

Don't break my heart.

"You don't have to do anything for me, Xander. I can take care of myself."

"I know you can. But that doesn't mean you should always have to. Let someone else have some of the burden sometime. You don't have to do everything, be everything for everyone."

"Yes, I do."

"Then let me make it easier for you. Trust me a little."

"Are you going to write me a check, Alex?"

His tone cooled ever so slightly. "Is that what you want?"

"No." She rolled over so that her cheek rested atop their laced hands. "I want this." *I want you.* She laughed softly at his hesitation. "The check would probably be easier." When he said nothing, she asked, "What do you want?"

"I want one of my pain pills. And then I want to fall asleep with you wrapped around me."

She pressed a kiss to his bare chest. "You don't want much."

"More than you know."

She pondered that over as she got his prescription bottle. What did he want that he couldn't buy ten times over? Except affection. And his stepfather's freedom.

She paused to check on her uncle, but Charley was no longer on the sofa. The service door was open and his battered Bronco was gone. Sighing, she went to close and lock the door. She was used to his melancholy when his thoughts turned to her father and those long-ago events. She empathized with his misery. She tried casting him in the role Xander was determined for him to play, but he didn't fit. He couldn't fit.

Xander had to be wrong. He had to be.

But looking at him when she returned to her bedroom, seeing the sharp intelligence in his gaze, the determined square of his chin, the methodical line of his mouth, she didn't see someone given to mistakes. Xander was careful, a cautious collector of details. He wouldn't make unfounded assumptions. He wouldn't be led down the wrong path by vague circumstance.

So where did that leave her? One of them had to be wrong? His head or her heart?

At the moment, his head was puckered with stitches and aching enough to make him squint. He washed down the pills with a cup of water she brought him then closed his eyes as if demanding instant relief. The same way he'd demand to know the truth of any given situation.

And what was she going to do if he implicated her uncle? Or her friends? Betray them by choice just to have him? Would she be that desperate for his company, for his kisses?

Xander glanced up as she continued to stand at the bedside, her expression filled with shadows. His smile leveled out into a thin line then began to take a downward turn. The welcoming light in his dark eyes flickered out as if pinched between thumb and finger. And without so much as moving an inch, she sensed his distancing retreat behind guarded gates.

"I told you it wouldn't be easy, Mel." He waited for some reassurance. When it didn't come, he asked emotionlessly, "Do you want me to go?"

"It's late."

That wasn't an answer and it didn't satisfy his question. Or his sudden anxiousness. "I'll leave."

But when he tried to sit up, her hands were on his shoulders, pressing firmly until he was flat on his back again. She stretched out along the unyielding length of him, tucking in close. He eased his arms about her in a wary, incremental advance until she sighed deeply and relaxed.

"This is nice, isn't it?"

"Yes," he answered softly, nuzzling her hair and expelling a huge gust of relief.

It didn't take much time for the meds to kick in. He held on to the feel of her, to his awareness of her for as long as he could, cherishing the closeness he'd never desired with another woman. Then dreaming of it. Of her whispering, impossibly, against his lips, "I love you, Alex. Don't leave me."

The morning was already warm and he was still pleasantly buzzing when the sound of a quiet footstep stirred Xander from his placid state. He slit an eye open then loosed a smile.

"Morning, Kyle. What are you doing here?"

"This was the first place I thought to look and the last place I wanted to find you." And he didn't look pleased.

"I had to pick up my other shoe."

"Is it under the covers?"

He wiggled bare toes. "Not at the moment." Putting on a repentant face, he confessed, "She took advantage of my injured and disoriented state."

Kyle snorted.

"And she enjoyed every minute of it. Good morning, Kyle."

The sight of Mel Parrish emerging from the bathroom in a hot pink bra and panties, looking not the least bit disconcerted, was worse then finding his best friend in her bed. But what truly alarmed him was the melting heat in Xander's eyes when he beheld her. After tugging on a pair of jeans and an olive drab T-shirt, Mel helped herself to a shamelessly long and complex feast off Xander's mouth, lifting up just far enough to promise, "I'll see you tonight."

"You be careful up there," he charged as his hands rubbed over the curve of her rump with obvious familiarity.

She kissed him again, a quick, hard press of passion then scrambled back out of his reach. The sight of Xander Caufield under her covers wasn't easy to walk away from. As she pulled her hair back into a rubber band and fed the ponytail through the back of her ball cap, she regarded Kyle D'Angelo soberly. He was dressed casually in a pair of scandalously snug jeans and sleeveless sweatshirt that displayed a variation on the same tattoo Xander had on his upper arm. His dark eyes were cool and disapproving as she moved around him. Until she touched his forearm and murmured, "Keep him safe."

No amount of smooching or hot glances could move Kyle D'Angelo's hardened heart the way that simple statement did. And that didn't make him any happier. After she'd gone, he regarded a very evasive Xander with a demand of, "Well?"

A quick flicker of his eyes, up then away. "Well, what?"

"Do you have a death wish or are you just working an angle?"

Something shifted subtly beneath Xander's impassive front, something dark and angry. "No," he said curtly to encompass both questions. His good-humored lethargy had disappeared behind a steely edge that was decidedly unfriendly.

"Did she tell you anything?"

"Nothing I'd care to share with you at the moment. Toss me my clothes."

Normally, Kyle would have lit into him for putting their plan at risk, for placing himself in the hands of the very people they were attempting to convict when he was so vulnerable. Vulnerable on more than one level. But something was different about this case, this woman, so he approached with extreme caution. Assuming a neutral pose, he watched Xander struggle to sit up then battle the challenge of putting on his pants when he couldn't lean over far enough to reach his feet and his knee wouldn't bend. Finally, he gave up in frustration to growl, "A little assistance here would be nice."

Without comment, Kyle helped him get dressed, and while Xander paled and sucked air, laced on his sloppy shoes. Then Kyle lingered for an awkward minute, crouched at his feet, carefully thinking out his words. "I hope you know what you're doing."

A small smile and weak laugh. "No. I really don't."

Kyle sighed. "Everything's set, Alex. If you want to pull the plug and back away, tell me now. This is your show. You call the shots. I'll go along with whatever you decide to do. No questions. No explanations needed."

And he would, Xander realized with a humbling certainty. With one word from him, his friend would abandon months of planning and hard work with the payoff so close they could taste it. With one word, Xander could absolve himself from having to make choices that were tearing his heart and soul to shreds and Kyle would never hold him accountable for it. What the hell had he ever done to deserve such loyalty?

Then he recalled a younger Kyle D'Angelo huddled on a ledge, shaking with cold and the first stages of shock but pushing him firmly away, saying, "You go. Go while you can. I'll be fine."

Xander drew a deep, steadying breath.

"Let's go see a man about a car."

Chapter 14

"Got company, One Night."

The shout drew her attention from the spread of maps and bottle of water she was gulping down. Quinn followed her gaze behind them and she vaguely heard his grumbled curse.

"We don't have time for this, Mel."

"I'll be just a second," she answered, already too distracted to really note his protest.

"Guess we'll have to think up a new nickname for you." He waved a hand to her visitor and hollered, "Hey, tough guy. Wanna toss that suit coat and crutches aside and go up with us?"

Xander responded with a faint smile as he angled out of the front seat of the Navigator to hop down on one leg. "Not today."

She was moving at a brisk trot when her eagerness met with the brick wall of awareness. He was dressed in an all-business suit, groomed, slick and enigmatic behind a pair of impenetrable dark glasses. Kyle D'Angelo was behind the wheel in similar intimidation garb, like the fabled Men in Black. He stared straight ahead. Mel slowed, the gladness that had lifted her spirit beginning to sink in apprehension. She was walking when she finally reached Xander, reluctance dragging her steps.

"Alex, what are you doing out here?"

He took down his dark glasses and her heart shuddered. His stare was as flat, black and uncompromising as the material of his suit. She placed her fingertips on his lapels in a gesture of supplication.

"Alex, what is it?" She knew, without him saying a word.

"We paid a visit to Petroni Auto."

She took a betrayal-lanced breath. "You said you wouldn't act on anything you learned from me."

"I said I wouldn't ask you any questions and I didn't."

That was just semantics. He'd learned about Sid Petroni while in her bed and it didn't get much more personal than that. Her hands curled in his coat. Her voice was low and rough. "What did you find out? Or can't you tell me that?"

"Xander, keep your mouth shut," Kyle warned somberly from inside the vehicle.

But Xander stared unflinchingly into her eyes, knowing what he was about to reveal would give her the power to bring their case crashing down. "Petroni has a black SUV loaner. With a crack in the windshield matching the one in my skull."

The significance buckled her knees. She shook her head, wishing she didn't understand it.

"Your uncle was using it while his vehicle was in the shop." Xander's hands came up to cover hers in a warm press. His expression never altered. "He gassed it up that morning in Tahoe. On the road back to Reno, he tried to run me off the side of a mountain then, outside your hangar, he tried to run me over."

Presented in such an inflectionless fashion, the truth was almost too much to absorb at one time. A bitter, acid taste burned in the back of her throat. She couldn't catch her breath. For the first time in her life, she feared she might faint. His grip strengthened, preparing to support her if he needed to. A soft, strangled sob finally escaped the compression of hurt, allowed a saving rush of oxygen to follow. And her thoughts began to race, quickly, frantically ahead.

"What are you going to do now?" Shades of meaning weighed her question.

"Alex." Again, the somber cautioning from his driver.

"I can't tell you that, Mel. You promised you wouldn't try to stop me." But he was watching the fear and desperation at work in her expression and he knew she couldn't keep her word.

"Alex, please don't."

His gaze dropped briefly, as if that could erase the anguish in her face or silence the agony in her plea. Nothing could. "I'm sorry, Melody." He met her tragic look and saw in those fierce depths the end of everything he was trying to cling to. "When this is done," he reminded her with a quiet intensity. Objection sparked in her narrowing stare.

"Why did you come here?"

What could he say? That he had to see her for what

he feared was the last time? "I didn't want it to blind-side you."

She winced at his impersonal delivery. "Better coming from you, is that it?"

"Yes." She started to pull her hands away but he wouldn't let her go. "We'll talk when this is over."

"I can't imagine what we'll have to say."

"Mel, I want to help you. I can help you."

Her glare cut like the cool flame of a TIG welder. "I think you've helped yourself to all you're going to, Xan-der." Her hands jerked free and he tensed, expecting her to plant the brunt of her upset across his face. But she aimed lower, her words tearing viscerally with a brutal slash. "I wish he'd killed you."

His lips pinched. "Maybe that would have been for the best." Slowly, he restored his wraparound glasses to present a blank front in the face of her fury. Watching her stalk away through glittery shards of remorse before getting back in the vehicle.

For the first fifteen minutes of the drive, there was ab-solute silence inside the Navigator. Kyle kept his attention on the twists and turns of the road while sparing covert glances for his passenger. Because of the wraparound sun-glasses, all he could see of Xander's expression was the immobile cut of his jaw and unsmiling set of his mouth. The only thing that betrayed any emotion at all was the way he was restlessly rubbing his knee.

"Alex?"

"There is no advice that you can give right now that I want to hear. So just keep it to yourself."

"I was going to ask if you needed anything for your knee."

"Oh." He sounded sheepish when he murmured, "No, it's fine. It gives me something to focus on."

The more manageable of what he was suffering from. Kyle understood so he offered, "This isn't how I wanted things to end up for you. You know that, don't you?"

"Sure."

Kyle frowned. Not exactly convincing. He checked the dashboard digital readout. "I'll drop off the money in about twenty. I want you to hang back and stay out of it."

"I think he already got a pretty good look at me while I was smashed up against his windshield like a bug."

Ignoring the sarcasm, he continued. "But he hasn't seen me, at least that we know of."

"Depending on what Mel's said." Xander spoke for them both.

"We don't know that she's told him anything."

Xander made an indecipherable sound.

I wished he'd killed you.

His stepfather's release had been the driving force of his days and nights. The means or costs hadn't mattered, not when compared to the weight of his guilt. Now that balance had taken an unexpected tip. And he found himself once again struggling against the whisper of doubt in the back of his mind.

What if his stepfather wasn't innocent? What if incarcerating Charley Parrish did nothing more than tear the stability out from under the woman who'd come to mean more to him than the life she now held so cheaply? Even as they swung into the empty parking lot, he knew it was too late to pull back. It was too late the second he'd seen that grill looming up behind his rental. The moment, frozen in time, when Mel said, "Please don't," knowing it had already been done. The only thing left was to ride it out all the way to the bittersweet end.

The passenger door opened. Kyle held out his hand. "Money?"

"What? I'm supposed to wait in the car? I don't pay for a ride I don't get to take."

"You're not up to this." Blunt and to the point.

"Don't tell me what I am."

Kyle put up his hands in a hold-me-harmless gesture. "She told me to keep you safe."

Pain gutted him. "I don't think she's going to hold you to that." He threw the bag of cash at his friend. "Let's do it."

Pride goaded Xander into approaching the situation on his own feet, but after cresting the top of the front steps without his crutches that arrogance was considerably humbled. "Where are we supposed to make our deposit?" His hope for nice and easy faded with Kyle's reply.

"Casino office up on four." He grinned at Xander's explicit response. "Far be it from me to pull the joy of the ride out from under you. C'mon. There's an elevator in back."

"Back" turned out to be about three thousand agonizing steps all trampling on the coattails of his empty bravado. Only to find the doors propped open with no sign of an elevator. And four flights of stairs. He stared up them in dismay then met Kyle's gaze.

"This is where reality hits the road, bro." He pointed to the bottom step. "Have a seat. I'll be back in a minute."

He didn't argue. "Be careful."

D'Angelo grinned. "Only take a few. Then we'll get this

place locked down tight and catch the bastard in the act."
He put a hand on his friend's shoulder and squeezed tight.
"Then we'll go get your dad."

Xander's gaze shifted to the floor, unable to express
himself with more than just a nod. He eased down to take
that bottom step, his leg stretched out in front of him to
give him some mild degree of relief. And he waited, listening to Kyle's quick footfalls as he jogged up the stairs,
taking those minutes to dare to imagine actually bringing
his stepfather home, being able to throw off the unbear-
ably heavy mantle of blame he'd worn for so many years
his shoulders were bowed beneath its weight. He couldn't
remember what it was like not to carry it.

But would knowing he'd exchanged his stepfather's un-
just punishment for Charley's freedom mean trading one
burden of guilt for another? The wounded fury in Mel's
eyes was carved upon his supposedly nonexistent soul.
Mel, what was I supposed to do?

From somewhere, several turns in the stairs above him, he
heard a loud thump then the unmistakable clatter of someone tumbling head over heels down the steps. Then silence.

"Kyle?"

Dammit.

"Kyle!"

He dragged himself to his feet and started up, hurrying,
movements growing halted, faltering as he relied on the
rails to pull him past each consecutive riser. By the time he
rounded the third landing, he was wringing wet and dizzy
with pain.

And then he saw Kyle D'Angelo sprawled at the next
half turn, one foot heading up, one hand trailing down.

Even as he moaned his friend's name in an agony of disbelief, Xander was aware of another subtle change in circumstance. One, more potentially devastating than the sight of Kyle's inanimate form.

Smoke, rising thick and strong up through the open stairwell.

She had no business being in the air.

Quinn took one look at her when she returned to the table, gripped her arm and marched her off to the side. She was barely holding it together. Her ribs hurt from suppressing the convulsive jerks of her chest. Quinn offered no sympathy. His reaction was all fierce male outrage.

"What did he do? Do you want me to break his other leg?"

She gave her head a brisk shake. "No. It's not him. It's nothing he's done."

"Oh, bull-ony. That boy's got you so turned inside out you can't even see where you're walking." The fact that she didn't argue alarmed him more than her pallor. "Mel, what's going on?"

"I have to go. I have some family things to take care of."

That immediately sobered him. "Is everyone all right? What can I do?"

She leaned into him, drawing strength from his uncompromising support. "I need to get home. I need to talk to Charley. If you see him, tell him to meet me at the hangar. It's important, Quinn."

"Go. We can't use you when you're distracted anyway. And if you decide you want me to kick the slats outta your pretty boyfriend, just let me know. Be happy to do it."

Running over Xander with a car wouldn't be Quinn

Naylor's style. He'd prefer a direct confrontation involving skinned knuckles and testosterone, not high-grade ethanol. But how would her uncle deal with him if he felt his family was being threatened? Quick, impersonal. And final.

She flew back to Reno, realizing even as she touched down that Charley was gone. The hangar door was open and the Shorts was missing. Was he walking right into Xander's coldly conceived trap? Should she warn him away? She thought of the single shoe lying on the tarmac and turmoil fisted cruelly about her heart. But Alex Caufield wasn't her problem anymore. Charley was.

She could hear the fax machine humming as she entered the stifling Quonset. She stopped to look at the information spitting out onto the floor. A quick scoop and shuffle of the pages showed them to be medical bills for Karen. Thousands upon thousands of dollars, all paid in full.

For you girls. I did it for you girls.

Oh, Charley, you fool.

Debts were a constant in their line of work. They'd always owe someone for something. And those debts would always be paid…eventually. When had he decided that buying the Long Ranger or sending Karen to art school was more important than living on a lower, leaner scale without the threat of imprisonment hanging over their heads? Or attempted murder? Why would he ever think running down Xander Caufield would be preferable to telling even such an ugly truth? What made him think she wouldn't have understood, even if she didn't condone, his actions? She could forgive him anything. And then in her tortured mind's eye, she saw, again, the discarded shoe with laces strewn.

Anything but that.

And that's when she realized with no little surprise how her priorities had just been reshuffled.

Trust me. Xander had offered his help and she had cut his knees out from under him. He hadn't created the situation. His reasons weren't self-serving or frivolous. They were no less noble than her own. But there was no honor in what she'd done to him. She'd shown not the slightest mercy.

I wish he'd killed you.

How could she have said such a thing? Surely, he wouldn't believe she meant it. And she saw again his small, shielding smile as he internally backed away.

"Oh, Alex, I'm sorry. Where are you? What are you doing?"

The phone rang, making her jump. She snatched up the receiver, stopping herself just short of saying his name.

"Mel?"

"Karen?"

"Sit down, baby. It's not good."

"What? Tell me."

"Some sparks got to a resort over on the east side of the lake. The Birches. It's fully engaged."

"So?"

"I just heard on the radio that Xander's trapped inside. They don't know if they can get to him in time. Mel? Did you hear me?"

She dropped the phone. She was running for the copter. The Birches. She knew the place, but what she couldn't figure was how the fire had reached it so fast. According to the weather data they'd gone over from just hours ago, there was no wind shift that would bring danger raining down upon that roof.

Arson.

The answer jumped out at her. That's why Xander was there and most likely Kyle D'Angleo as well. There to trap Charley. Only from the sound of it, they were the ones who'd been caught.

It took long agonizing minutes to pop up out of the Reno basin and arrow toward Tahoe. She tried not to think about what she might find but adrenalin was already pumping through her system, making her pulse rock and her hand remarkably steady.

I'm on my way, Alex. Hang on. Be safe.

The Birches was an ambitious place, set high up off the beaten tourist path. A central tower of rooms rose eight stories, flanked by low wings. The building was cut into a rock wall, accessible only by winding roads. She made a skimming pass, low enough to see the glow of flames behind the fronting of glass but no exterior evidence of fire. Not yet. Which may have explained why there were no crews on site. Just D'Angelo's big Navigator parked in the lot out front.

She made a quick call to dispatch, anticipating the grim news that all crews were too far away to provide an immediate assist. It would be up to her for the next crucial half hour.

She took another quick spin around the exterior. From what she could see, the fire was contained on the lower floors of the main tower and that's where she would find Xander and Kyle, right in the heat of things. There was no place for her to safely set down except on the roof of one of the wings, something Quinn would undoubtedly find reckless to the extreme. That would give her a few precious minutes to assess the situation and effect a rescue. Providing she could find the two men and a potential arsonist somewhere within the burning building. Inside. Where the flames leaped and consumed everything in their path.

Where she would have to go to find them.

She touched down without any problem. The problem arose when she had to step out and leave the safety of her bird behind. She forced herself to focus on Xander, inside, perhaps in need of her assistance. She couldn't let him down. Not over a little thing like mindless, dry-mouthed panic. She'd been more afraid of his first kiss than this long-overdue confrontation. Or so she tried to convince herself.

Part of the roof was constructed for an outdoor garden and restaurant. A pleasant, intimate place to view the distant lake and inhale the pungent scent of the firs. Pleasant when it wasn't about to become an inferno. A half-dozen sets of French doors that would stand open to guests were locked tight against her uninvited entry. Without hesitation, she picked up one of the heavy concrete planters and flung it through the glass. Carefully she unlatched the door and that's when it reached her. The stench of smoke.

Mel, help me!

She closed her eyes against the sickening wave of remembrance. Had her mother been conscious when the flames reached her? Had she cried out to be rescued as Karen had done? Calling for her. Pleading for her. Had she felt those first vicious tongues of fire or had the smoke mercifully spared her all that pain? How many nights had she woken in a sweat tormented by unanswerable questions? Would she be wondering over Xander the same way? Would the memory of the fire whirl that chased through her dreams now wear his face?

Not if she crossed that threshold.

The interior was wreathed in smoke—thick, undulating ropes of it snaking down the halls, a curtain of it muting the red glare of the fire in the rooms beyond. And Mel knew a moment of perfect terror.

She couldn't go any farther. She absolutely could not.

Heat rippled about her, drying her skin, burning her nose and eyes. How much worse must it be in the tower where the flames raced gleefully up floor by floor? How was she supposed to find survivors in that scorching maze? How was she supposed to save Xander? She'd have to go room to room, floor to floor.

And then, as her frantic gaze cast about in hopes of a solution, she hit upon one so simple and obvious she could only stare for a long blank moment. Then she lifted the receiver on the wall phone.

"If anyone can hear me, pick up the house phone." Her voice echoed eerily above the snap and pop of the fire. "Pick up the house phone if you can hear me."

She waited, heart pounding, breath shivering noisily. And finally, a flash of light on one of the lines.

"Mel?"

The bottom fell out of her stomach. "Alex, where are you?"

His voice sounded distant, hoarse and so damned good. "In the casino office on four. I was trying to make a call but none of the outside lines will work."

"Are you all right?"

"I was hit by a car, you know."

Her laugh wobbled. "I know. Can you get out? You have to get out now."

He was grim. "Kyle's in the stairwell. He's hurt. Bad."

"The fire?"

"No."

She didn't ask for more details. "You have to get out of there."

"I can't carry him and I won't leave him."

Her heart shuddered at that firmly spoken fact. And before she had a chance to think, she was saying, "I'll come to you."

"No. There's no way. Everything's burning below us. You wouldn't get through. Don't try, Mel. Promise me you won't."

Her mind worked furiously, scrambling over the detours and roadblocks trying to clear a rescue path. He couldn't come down, but he could go up.

"I've got the Long Ranger. If you can get to the roof—"

He sounded so calm, so reasonable. "There's no way I could get Kyle up four flights of stairs. I don't even know if I could make it on my own."

"You can make it. I know you can. The rescue units are coming. They're less than a half hour out. You come up and they'll go back for your friend. Alex, you come up."

Silence, then a quiet, "I'll wait with him."

"There's no time for this," she all but screamed into the phone. "Get yourself to the roof."

"We'll be on four, waiting. Tell them to hurry."

"Alex, please!"

"Mel, I can't go to his family and tell them I walked out of here and left him behind. He did this for me. For me. Don't you understand?" His voice fractured and fell off.

Of course she understood. She understood perfectly that he was going to die if he stayed where he was.

"Alex, you listen to me. Are you listening? Are you?"

"Yes."

"You get to those stairs, and I don't care how you do it, you get the both of you up to that roof. I can only wait about fifteen minutes. Do you understand? That's all the time I'll have." That's all the time he'd have. "Alex, can you hear me?"

"Yes."

"Get to the roof. Go now."

Silence.

"Don't make me have to go to both your families to tell them I left you behind." Her voice broke, snagging on the raw agony of circumstance. Then, because all she could envision was his small, tight smile, she told him, "You know I didn't mean what I said to you. You know that, right?"

A pause, then softly, "Right."

"Dammit, Alex, if you cheat me out of one more night, I will go into hell, itself, to bring you back. Now you move. You get to that roof and I'll be there. I'll be there for you. Go now."

"I'm sorry, Mel. I never meant for you to be hurt."

Her blood froze. "Alex! Don't you do this to me! Don't you dare quit on me!"

Another pause and softer still, "I love you, Mel."

"Alex!"

Then the connection was lost.

Chapter 15

He slid down the last few steps on his rump, injured leg no longer able to support him. Four flights. What a thing to ask.

Kyle was still unconscious, no help to him at all. But Xander was sure what he'd say if asked if he was ready to suffocate in the stairwell at Lake Tahoe. *Get me out of here, Xander. We've got a hot tub, booze and cigars waiting.* And two women they loved whether they'd had the guts to admit it or not.

I love you, Mel. What a selfish thing to do, leaving her with those last words. And coward that he was, he'd never have to do anything about it. Would never have to prove it to her. Every day. Every night, until they lost count.

I love you, Alex. Don't leave me. Had she said that or was it part of his drug-induced dreams? He hadn't had the chance to ask. And now he'd never know.

He wiped at his eyes. They burned and watered from the smoke that was rapidly contaminating their air supply. Fifteen minutes. The rest of his life condensed into that small capsule of time. Thirteen minutes now. He rubbed at the grinding ache in his knee and looked up the open stairwell. Sixty seconds per turn. Plenty of time. If he could move.

And what would happen at the end of that window of opportunity? Was Mel going to just fly away and leave them to the flames? No. *I will go into hell, itself.*

That realization scared him more than the heat and haze building around him. He knew exactly what she would do. She'd set the chopper back down and she'd come for him. She'd push her way into the merciless heart of the fire, without a thought to consequence, conquering her crippling fears, damning the odds just to get to him. Because whether she said it or not, she loved him. It was what he would do if their roles were reversed.

He couldn't let her make that foolish sacrifice. Not because he wasn't worth it. But, rather because she was worth too much.

Twelve minutes.

Cursing, he shoved himself up off the floor. Hobbling into the interior hallway, he searched for what he needed, a heavy panel of drapes and a restroom. Because he didn't know how close the flames were going to come in the next handful of minutes, he stuffed the curtains into the sink, wetting them piece at a time, then putting his head under the cold shock of water, soaking his hair and shirtfront. He'd shed his coat as the heat intensified. Dragging the drapes back to where he'd left his friend, he bent awkwardly to tie off one end then rolled the limp, dead weight of Kyle D'Angelo into them. If he couldn't carry him, perhaps he could haul him.

He backed up the stairs, dragging Kyle behind him. Don't think about the numbers, about the odds he would never recommend anyone to accept. He scooted back across the first landing. Three to go.

"Dammit, Kyle, you pudgy bastard. No more beer for you."

He was panting hard, trying to wring something useful from the thick scorched air. *Move.* He started counting the steps leading upward, dividing them down into how many seconds per riser, per section, per floor. *Move.* Two more. *Don't you leave me, Mel. Don't you leave me.* Push, pull. Push, pull. He continued up, pushing off with his good leg, dragging Kyle the way he'd pull on crew oars. Around the final two turns to the door leading to the roof. He leaned back against the service door, gasping, woozy with pain and lack of oxygen.

"You're going to owe me for this, D'Angelo. You're standing up with me at my wedding. I'll expect one hell of a bachelor party. Dom and dancing girls." The image of Mel Parrish swiveling her hips on a barroom table cauterized his thoughts. "Never mind the girls." Mel could dance for him on their wedding night.

Getting up off the floor was harder than crawling up four flights of stairs. His leg buckled, cramping in agony as he clung to the bar handle and pushed. The flood of fresh air sent him into a fit of coughing. Not just air, but air agitated by rotor wash. He managed to wave one arm then bent to haul Kyle across the threshold, muttering, "God, I love that woman," to his senseless friend.

It took a ridiculously long and painful moment to buckle into the harness, another minute of awkward struggle to secure Kyle's uncooperatively lax form. Then they were pulled off the resort roof. Xander didn't expel his breath until he rolled Kyle into the interior of the Bell and closed the door behind them.

And because the first thing she shouted back was, "Is he all right?" Xander knew he would love her forever.

"Fine. We both are. Go."

He collapsed on the floor of the helicopter, content to leave the driving to her. With one hand on his friend's chest to feel its reassuring rise and fall, Xander let his awareness of all else fade, becoming the vibration beneath him and the fierce ache pulsing through him. Then he felt a gentle touch on his face and heard the soft call of his name, coaxing him to open his eyes. Mel's worried features swam into view, but it was so hard to focus until Kyle D'Angelo was being pulled out from under his hand. He dragged himself up onto his elbows to caution, "You be careful of him. I didn't bounce his head off four flights of stairs to let you drop him."

Mel captured his hand and squeezed tight as one of the attendants spoke to her.

"Your call said one injury. Does he need the E.R., too?"

"I need a wheelchair and a morphine drip."

"Shush. He was hit by a car. A wheelchair would be nice."

As they were settling him into the chair next to the gurney holding his friend, the sight of them immobilizing Kyle with a backboard and cervical collar stirred a new urgency.

"Is he going to be all right? Kyle? I want to go with him."

"What kind of insurance does he have? Are you family?"

"Yes, I'm family. Mel, get me his wallet. He's B-positive.

No allergies. He's got a previous back injury." He took the wallet, its leather grain still warm, and started fumbling through the plastic photo sleeves. Coming to a complete halt at the sight of a tattered ten-year-old candid photo of the two of them grinning widely, heads helmeted, displaying newly tattooed biceps and thumbs up after making a zip line through the jungle in Mexico. Xander tried to take a breath and couldn't. Driver's license, road service and credit cards spilled out onto his lap as his hands started shaking. "Mel, help me here." His eyes were suddenly, embarrassingly, too full to see what he was doing.

She knelt down and took the wallet, shuffling through it briefly to find the health insurance card, passing it up to one of the orderlies. Wordlessly, she put her arms about Xander and directed his head to her shoulder, holding him there while he gulped for air and composure. He tried to lift up at the sound of the gurney moving but she wouldn't let him.

"He's all right, Alex. How about you? How are you doing?"

"I got hit by a car, Mel," he mumbled, his voice thick, choked and nearly unrecognizable. She turned her face into the dark muss of his hair, breathing in smoke, her arms tightening protectively, just holding him for a long, silent moment. Then it passed. She could feel him gathering from whatever reserves he had left, building on them until he had the strength to lean away, his attention shifting from the two of them to the entrance to the hospital. She forced her hands to relax, her arms to open. And she stood away from him, moving to grip the handles of the wheel-chair. "Let's go find your friend."

They were directed to a quiet, sunny waiting room where they found a hard-cushioned sofa away from the other distracted occupants waiting for news. Mel brought him a large foam cup of ice water that he took gratefully, drinking deeply then dipping his fingers into the cold liquid to rub it soothingly over his eyes before slumping forward, elbows on thighs, head hanging low. A tremendous breath moved his shoulders and moved Mel in a way she hadn't thought possible. The need to reach out to him was complicated by caution, because of the words they'd exchanged. Hers to him in anger, his to her in confession. And then there was the awkward weight of what hadn't been said, the things she was afraid to hear. Finally, she had to know.

"What happened?"

"Everything that could possibly go wrong. The lack of proper backup. My fault. He knew we were setting him up and he was ready for us. Bashed Kyle's head in with a fire extinguisher and took the money, using the fire to cover his tracks. I'm not blaming you for that, Mel."

Of course he was.

"I never said anything to him about you, Alex. Not that I wouldn't have. I just never had the chance."

He nodded, not looking at her, not doubting her, but that wasn't the same as not blaming her. Misery rose, a bitter tide.

"I sorry I didn't believe you sooner. I guess I just couldn't accept it until I saw all these bills this morning." She pulled the wadded stack of Karen's hospital invoices out of her back pocket to stare at them through a cloudy gaze. "Why couldn't he have said something to me. We could have figured something out. Something. Anything."

His hand eased over the back of hers, fingers pushing

between hers to curl into a comforting clasp. "Maybe he just couldn't get past his pride, Mel. It's hard for a man to admit that he's not in control of things that matter to him."

He glanced up at her then, his gaze not exactly guarded but not an open book, either. Whatever else he might have said went unvoiced when his bean-counter brain was engaged by the long list of numbers in her hand. "May I see those?"

She watched him scan the pages, devouring the information they contained. Not knowing what to make of it.

"Where did you get this?"

"Off our fax this morning. Why?"

His reactions had closed ranks around whatever whirred through his mind. She couldn't decipher anything beyond a mild puzzlement. "Xander, what is it?"

Before she could question him further, they were approached by one of the hospital staff who asked, "You brought in Mr. D'Angelo?"

"Yes." Xander started to stand, but the sudden wrenching pain dropped him back into his seat. Clutching his knee, he demanded, "Is he all right? Can I see him?"

"Probably not for a couple of hours. We've got some more tests to run. He's got a hard head, but his back has some interesting stuff going on in it and we just want to make sure."

Xander's expression became a stark blank. "Oh my God. Was it something I did dragging him up those stairs? I didn't think—I didn't think."

"You saved his life. The bumpy ride probably didn't help but it didn't hurt that much, either."

Xander nodded stiffly, not sure he believed it.

The resident frowned slightly. "What about you?" He

had Xander by the chin and was flashing his pocket light in this eyes without waiting for an answer. Then he checked the stitches in his brow. "Some of our work?"

"I'm recommending you to all my friends."

"And following up with your primary-care physician?"

"Of course."

The resident scowled suspiciously then challenged Mel. "You make sure he does."

She could have said she had no idea where Xander Caufield would keep such an individual, but her cell phone saved her from that embarrassment.

"Melody?"

"Quinn, what's wrong?" He never, ever called her by her full name. The fact that he chose to do so now put a terrible fear in her.

"Is anyone with you?"

"Xander's here. Why?"

"Let me talk to him for a second."

Xander nodded to the resident and took the phone, alerted by Mel's rigid posture. "Yes?" He listened impassively for a moment, his eyes not quite making contact with hers. Then he turned away so the next low exchanges couldn't be overheard. She touched his arm, the quick bunch of tension confirming the worst.

Whatever it was, it was bad.

She struggled to maintain a neutral face when he closed the phone and turned to her. Searching for clues in his expression was like looking for elusive handholds on a rock wall.

"Alex?" she prompted softly.

"I was wrong, Mel. About everything. I'm sorry."

"Wrong about what?"

"Quinn was calling from the site of a small-plane crash. They're still looking for the pilot. He'd been running hot-shots early this morning and he went down in a bank of fog. Mel, it's Charley."

She blinked then shook her head. "That's impossible. He can't fly anymore, not with his health history. There must be some mistake."

"No mistake. I wish there was."

Tears flooded up into her eyes, making Xander's somber visage shimmer. She managed to swallow down the sobs that threatened. "Does Karen know?"

"Quinn was hoping you and I could tell her and wait with her." Something dark and shadowed flickered in the back of his gaze. "Unless you think it would be inappropriate for me to be there...all things considered."

She stared at him blankly, unable to comprehend the objection. "Not if it will make you feel uncomfortable."

He cursed low and soft and reached out to draw her up against him, letting her lean into him, tense and shivering. "It's not about me, Mel. I'll be there if you want me to be."

"I want you there."

"Okay."

"What about Kyle?"

"He's in good hands. I want to make sure you are, too."

At that moment, she wanted nothing more than to melt into him, into his heat and strength and surprisingly stalwart support. The circle of his arms and the hard wall of his chest were intimately familiar. She no longer struggled against the desire to surrender to the comfort she found there. She knew if she tipped back her head, he would kiss her, deeply, sweetly, with a pulse-altering delight. And maybe he would say those words again, those heartbreaking words he'd said to her over the phone when he'd thought they'd never see each other again. And if he said them, maybe she would be foolish enough to repeat that sentiment, and even though she'd mean it, that wouldn't make it the right or the smart thing to do. Not now. Not yet.

She sat back, the separation gradual, the movement reluctant until only her palms lingered flush upon his chest. She felt his focus upon her face but couldn't raise her own to meet it.

"Mel?"

Slowly, his hand scooped under her chin, his fingertips grazing light and warm along the curve of her cheek, coaxing her to look up at him. His expression going still when she did and he could read the awful fright and hesitancy in hers. His hand withdrew. His promise was low and fiercely sincere.

"I won't let you down."

They were back in the air, skimming for Tahoe within minutes. Xander sat in the co-pilot's seat, keeping to the private turmoil of his thoughts while hers raced wildly.

Why would Charley take the plane up when he knew the results could be disastrous? It was her father all over again. Foolish, reckless and now most likely dead, too. The same feelings of helplessness and anger swamped the underlying sense of sorrow.

"How could he do this to me, to Karen?" Mel was only vaguely aware she was speaking out loud. Xander remained silent, knowing she wasn't addressing him or expecting a response. "What will we do without him? How am I going to manage our company? Damn you, Charley. You were all we had left."

"Mel, I'm—"

She turned on him in an irrational rage because he was within striking range. "Sorry? Don't you dare say you're sorry. You don't know anything. You don't know what it's like just waiting for everyone you love to leave you."

He was staring out the window, the back of his head to her when he answered in a low, flat tone. "You're right. I wouldn't know anything about that."

But of course he would. He would know everything about it.

Her temper blew out to a deep, anguished ache. "Alex—"

"Don't apologize to me, Mel. There's no need."

There was every need because she'd hurt him without reason. After he'd left the only person in the world who meant anything to him to be with her, for no reason other than…what? Because he cared? Or because without Charley Parrish as his main suspect, he was back at square one? She hadn't thought that far ahead. But glancing over at his averted features, at the stiff set of his posture, she knew he had. He was way ahead of her, weighing circumstance and consequence and his next move even as she was reconciling her life to another terrible loss.

She brought the Long Ranger down with a light touch at Karen's. Then she turned at the feel of Xander's light touch beneath her jaw. When he leaned toward her, she didn't draw back, but neither did she move to meet his soft, seeking kiss. Tasting her uncertainty, he whispered against her mouth, "That's for when I thought I'd never have the chance to kiss you again."

She stared into his eyes, mesmerized by the deep hints of green beneath the long dark fringe of lashes, by the hint of emotions so deep and complex, she couldn't begin to guess at them because they reflected her own. She touched his cheek, tracing those glorious angles, sketching beneath the fading pallet of colors beneath the one eye, brushing his glossy hair back from the neat line of stitches.

"Thank you for being here with me."

And there it was, the slight shift in the focus of his gaze, easing from direct contact. But not with guilt. With something else she couldn't quite identify.

"Let's go. I'm sure Karen is wondering why we're here."

But Karen wasn't waiting on the porch or in the taste-fully welcoming interior of her home. Slowed by the burden of Xander hobbling at her side using her shoulder for a crutch, Mel crossed the smooth sand-colored tiles, heading for Karen's studio.

Karen's wheelchair was angled toward the studio, inexplicably empty.

Fearing something had happened to her cousin, Mel started forward only to be checked by the tight curl of Xander's arm.

"Wait."

She didn't understand. And then she heard the scuffle of footsteps. Karen wasn't alone. A pair of braided leather sandals appeared in the doorway beneath the sway of a gauzy patterned skirt. It took Mel a moment to process what she was seeing.

Karen Parrish was standing in the doorway.

Chapter 16

"So surprised." Karen's smile mocked her cousin's incredulous expression. Then she turned to Xander. "But not you. I knew you were going to be a problem the second I laid eyes on you. Too smart. When did you figure it out?"

"A recent development. Apparently not quite smart enough."

"You've been breathing down my neck for a long time. That was you, wasn't it? Asking questions, digging into our business? This time you just got a little too close for comfort. Sorry about running you over. Nothing personal."

"That depends on which side of the windshield you're on."

She laughed out loud. "I like you, Xander." Then her mood sobered. "What gave me away?"

"The medical bills. I'm guessing your father had them faxed to him. When did he find out?"

Her expression toughened. "I think it's been sneaking up on him for some time but, like Mel, he didn't want to believe it."

Mel's confused gaze jumped between the two of them. Xander stood back, distancing himself from her, his expression taut, blank, dangerously calm. Karen…this was a Karen she didn't recognize. She'd been behind the wheel of the vehicle that struck Xander. She'd been behind the arsons, not Charley. Those truths swirled behind the one huge shock she had yet to conquer.

"You can walk. How? For how long?"

"I didn't go to art school for two years. I went to a specialized burn center on the East Coast to have reparations to muscle and tissue. And then month after month of physical therapy. You can't imagine what that was like."

Her eyes welled up, imagining. "Why didn't you tell us?"

Her voice lowered to a harsh rumble of pain and anger. "You left me, Mel. You left me to burn."

"No!"

"After what I did for you, for us, and you ran. You ran."

A quiet horror began to spread. "What did you do, Karen?"

"She was going to him, Mel. They were going to run away together and leave us behind, just like my mother did."

"Who?"

"Your mother, my father."

"What?"

"They were having an affair, you fool. For years, off and on, between your father's flings. Charley wanted her to leave him but she wouldn't, until that last night. I heard her talking to Charley, telling him that she'd given Paddy an ultimatum, that if he didn't come to get us in the morning, she was going to walk away from him for good. That's where we were going. She was going to meet Charley and they were going to leave together. And where do you think that would have left us, Mel? Where?"

As shocked as she was to have the ugly facts pushed into her face, those truths made an unpleasant sense to Mel. Her mother turning from the fiery, hurtful relationship with her father to find comfort with his always-empathetic brother. The damaging cycle of repentance, forgiveness and fractured faith slowly wearing her down until only resentment remained. And escape. But Karen was very wrong about one thing.

"She never would have left us behind. Never."

Karen's glittering eyes narrowed. "That's because I didn't give her the chance."

"Karen, what did you do?" Mel asked again, dreading the answer that would rip the rest of her family apart.

"She went inside to find Charley. But she didn't realize that I knew what they were planning. She looked just as surprised as Xander's friend when I met her on the stairs. It just happened. I didn't plan to kill her." She shrugged with a nonchalance that froze Mel to the soul. "But it worked out for the best. We'd have Charley and Paddy and all I had to do was cover up what I'd done. I'd never set a fire before. It was my first and almost my last. Because you ran. Just like my mother. Just like yours and Charley were planning to do."

"Oh, my God." Mel reeled back, desperately needing to sit down, to cling to something…someone. But Xander offered nothing but an emotionless stare and an impartial stance. And subtly, a warning, his hands pressing down slightly on air, advising her, silently, to keep things under control. She took a deep breath. "I couldn't reach you, Karen. I went for help. And they saved you. Because I went for help, you're alive."

And in saying that out loud to convince her cousin, she was finally able to convince herself. She'd done nothing wrong. She wasn't responsible for her mother's death or Karen's injuries.

"You saved me." Karen's laugh was hard and awful. "What you left me was not living. I was in hell. A monster. The way Charley looked at me that first time. He didn't think I could see, but I did. The horror in his face. Because I was alive and she wasn't. And he resented every penny he gave up for my sake."

"Karen, how can you say that? You know that's not true."

But she continued on, bitterness oozing from every word, pain twisting her heart the way the scars marred her skin. "Why would he give everything up for damaged goods? When he had you. Her daughter. He couldn't even look at me, Mel."

"Charley loves you, Karen. We both do."

"And you, you who promised you'd always be there for me. Where were you, Mel? Where were you when I was burning? You saved yourself. You wouldn't go into the fire for me. But you would for him." She stabbed an accusing finger at Xander. Her voice quivered with hurt and rage. "You did for him. Why do you think I called you? I wanted to see if you would go. I wanted to see if you would make that sacrifice for a near stranger who shared your sheets when you wouldn't for family. For me. Knowing he betrayed you, you would have gone into the fire for him."

She didn't spare Xander a glance to gauge his reaction. She didn't dare. "Yes. Because I'm not twelve anymore, Karen. I'm not that helpless, frightened child. I'm sorry if I wasn't ready to die for you then. But I couldn't save you and I wanted you to live. I didn't want to lose you. You were my family. You are my family. And I don't want to lose you now. Let me help you."

"Now you want to help me. Well, it's a little late for that. I've had to help myself. Paddy showed me how."

"What?"

"Oh, not intentionally. He was talking about how some casino owner had contacted him and asked if he would be interested in paying off some of his debt by setting a convenient fire. Paddy, being shortsighted, was indignant, but I saw the potential. And I made my first deal. The money paid for my legs. It gave me the promise of a new life. After that, it got easy."

"Like my father's hotel." Xander intruded into the conversation with a quiet conclusion.

She met his gaze unapologetically. "That paid off very well."

"With a man's life."

"That wasn't intentional. He got greedy. He wanted to change the terms at the last minute. That was unacceptable."

"And my father?"

"I guess it doesn't matter if you know. He wasn't involved. Sorry he got left holding the bag, but it wasn't like I could testify on his behalf."

Xander's eyes closed briefly but opened backlit with determination. "Do you have any proof that he wasn't involved?"

"I have the security tape from the hotel office. It captures your father's partner setting up the entire thing. And he specifically states that your father did not know anything about our arrangement. He had some fairly unflattering things to say about you, too. Only, of course, I didn't make the connection then."

"Would you give it to me?"

"Why would I want to do that?"

"Because you're not as coldhearted as you pretend to be. If you were, there wouldn't be such warmth in your paintings. If you were, you wouldn't have tried so hard to protect Mel from me. Tell me that's not part of the reason you wanted to run me down. Because I lied to her. Because I hurt her. And you wanted me to pay for that, just like you wanted Charley to pay for hurting you. He was surprised, wasn't he, when you told him that morning?"

"Oh, yes." She smiled. "Surprised and hurt and guilty, for betraying his brother, for betraying me. He said he would make it up to me by taking the blame for everything I'd done. He even let me borrow the SUV."

"But there was just one problem, wasn't there?"

"You. You and Mel. You used her to set a trap for me. You made her suspicious. You got her asking questions. And here you are. What am I going to do with you?"

"Karen," Mel began in an anguished voice, "Charley's—"

"Going to take the fall for you," Xander interrupted smoothly. A quick flash of his eyes warned her to keep quiet. "That should satisfy your need to punish everyone."

Karen studied him for a long moment. "Not quite."

In that instant, Mel saw everything all too clearly. Karen wanted to hurt her and she would use Xander to exact that pain. She'd killed. She wouldn't hesitate, because she had nothing to lose. Whereas Mel held everything in the balance. Particularly the man bargaining with a madwoman for his father's freedom. Both Karen and Xander would do whatever necessary to achieve their goal, recklessly, without thought, without care or caution. So Mel would have to do whatever she could to keep them safe. And that meant taking Xander out of the equation.

"You were right, Karen. You were right all along. About him. About Charley and my father."

Xander's gaze cut to her in a quick impassive flicker as Karen weighed her cousin's response suspiciously.

"You were right, Karen. There's no percentage in loving a man like him. He doesn't understand the concept. It's all about business. And he's very, very good at what he does. This isn't his concern, so give him what he wants and let him leave so we can get on with our family business, just you and me."

"Just like that. Let him go. He's not going to care if I keep his money."

"It's not about the money. He has plenty of that. He doesn't care enough about anyone or anything else to meddle in our affairs. It's all about what he wants. He'll just walk away. Isn't that right, Alex?"

He examined the hard lines of her face, his own inscrutable. She'd called him Alex not Xander. Would he catch the significance? *Come on, smart guy. Don't let me down.*

His reply was glacial. "I just want to get my father out of prison. I don't give a damn about you people and your problems."

He could have been telling the truth.

"Don't complicate things, Karen," Mel soothed gently. "It can stop here. It doesn't have to end badly."

"Badly." Karen mused over that for a moment. "No, I suppose it doesn't."

"You were just thinking of me. I understand that now. You were taking care of me, of both of us. That's what you've been doing, all along. Paying the bills, making sure we had what we needed. Something Paddy never did. Something Charley couldn't handle. It's always been just the two of us. We don't need anyone else. Give him what he wants, Karen. I'll stand by you the way I should have done all those years ago." Tears glistened in her eyes. "I won't let you down."

Slowly, Karen took a videotape from the deep pocket of her skirt and extended it to Xander. "Take it and go."

Xander reached out and took the tape from her. He turned it over and over in his hands, regarding it through an oddly opaque stare. Clutching it to his chest, he looked up at Mel with a scary intensity. Something was very wrong. He put out his hand.

"Mel, come say goodbye to me."

She didn't move. "Goodbye, Alex."

The strange starkness in his eyes kept getting bigger until Mel finally recognized the expression. She hadn't seen it when he had confronted armed muggers. Not when he'd stepped out of her helicopter. Why now? Why did he look so deeply, mortally afraid?

"Mel, come here to me."

When she took a step toward him, Karen's hand closed about her wrist. Hard. She glanced down at the fierce grip then up at Xander in question. But his focus was her cousin.

"Karen, don't do this. Please.

"Alex?"

"She would never trust me to walk out of here and say nothing, Mel. So it must not matter. Why doesn't it matter?"

Karen's smile was sad. "Why do you have to be so clever? Just go. You've got what you wanted."

"But I don't. Karen, please don't take her with you."

"Karen? Where are we going?"

"Not far, Mel. It won't hurt."

She reached into her pocket again. And drew out a remote detonator. Mel froze.

"I know about Charley," Karen said softly. "Quinn called me. He was so…concerned. I asked him to send you over to stay with me. It just got too out of control, Mel. Charley trying to make amends. Xander trying to soothe his conscience. Quinn suffering so foolishly from unrequited love. We don't need them, Mel." Then fiercely, "They'll be sorry."

"This is about Quinn?"

"He's the only man I've ever wanted. The surgery was all scheduled. I was going to be beautiful again. And then Quinn would have looked at me the way he looks at you, but you ruined that for me. You knew how much I wanted him and you took him anyway, even though you didn't want him for yourself. First Charley, then Quinn. You just had to have it all. And now neither of us has anything."

"Karen, you're wrong. We still have each other. I love you. I would do anything for you. I would give my life for you." Her hand slipped over the one holding the detonator, trying to keep calm, to control the moment for just a little longer.

"Alex, go. Now." When he hesitated, she turned on him angrily, shouting, "Don't be stupid. It was just sex. I don't care about you. Go see to your family and let me take care of mine. I don't want you here. This doesn't involve you."

Still, he didn't move.

And then a large hand closed over hers and Karen's, holding them fast.

"Don't do nothing dumb, ladies. I don't want to have to clean up the mess."

Gingerly, Quinn relieved a startled Karen of the detonator, quickly disarmed it and then stepped back so her father could come in off the patio to sweep her up in his arms. Charley Parrish, scraped and bruised and openly weeping, hugged his daughter as she sagged to her knees, sobbing hysterically, clinging to the father she thought she'd lost.

"I would never leave you, Karen," he vowed. "The same way June would never leave Paddy. He was the one she was going to that day, not me. And I won't leave you now. Not ever."

Mel numbly followed Quinn's nod of acknowledgment to Xander.

"You knew he was all right?" she accused in quiet disbelief. "You knew and you let me think—"

Xander regarded her unblinkingly. "Charley told Quinn everything. That's what we were talking about on the phone at the hospital. It was our chance to draw her out, to get her to confess before the police were involved. I didn't know how it was going to play out, Mel."

"You doubted me. So you played me." Nothing had ever wounded quite so deeply.

"He's a right smart fellow, our pal Alex. Had everything

figured. Only you were supposed to wait for us, tough guy. You didn't have to go Lone Ranger. What's the use in having friends if you don't trust 'em to watch your back?" Quinn said.

Mel glanced down at the tape he held, her expression stiffening. "He had other priorities, Quinn. Xander doesn't understand trust or love." And she turned away from him, kneeling down to embrace her uncle and cousin.

Regarding his stoic rival with a pitying sigh, Quinn said, "Your friend's awake and asking after you. Grumbling something about you calling him a pudgy bastard."

Xander nodded, taking a step back, away from these people who no longer had room for him within their tight circle. He got as far as the front door, moving out of the way to let several police officers pass. Then found himself confronted by a hard-eyed man who demanded, "Are you Caufield? The name's Jack Chaney. My wife is Kyle D'Angelo's sister."

Xander smiled faintly. "Is she here to shoot him?"

"No, she sent me. She'd be here herself, but she's going to give birth in a couple of weeks and I don't trust her with weapons. Kyle sent me to pick you up. He ID'd Karen Parrish. I've got a charter jet waiting to take us to Colorado to make statements. You're all packed. Ready to go?"

"Alex!"

He staggered as Mel catapulted into his arms.

"Don't…" Her voice choked off.

"Don't what?" he urged as she clung to him, holding to her with everything he had, on every level he could, because for a moment, when her hand was on the detonator, she'd been ready to sacrifice herself for him. And it hadn't been part of her job.

"Don't forget me."

She pulled back abruptly, not saying anything more to relieve his anxiety. And she was gone.

Chapter 17

Xander heard the door open behind him. It took a long, agonizing moment for him to find the courage to turn toward the man standing there. They regarded each other, almost as if they were strangers. He looked good, lean, strong. Older. That's all he could tell before his eyes brimmed up, obscuring his vision. It took another torturous second for him to find his voice, a flat, impersonal tone that blacktopped over the cracks in his emotional surface.

"Your attorney's filed all the motions and has a hearing set for next week. He's confident you'll be out that afternoon."

"You'll be at the hearing?" A tenuous hope.

"If you want me to be."

"I'd like that. This was your doing, after all."

His features tightened into an impenetrable blank. "I know." He took a ragged breath. "I'm sorry."

"Alex, my being here wasn't your fault. I didn't blame you. I made some bad choices, depended on the wrong people."

"I'm sorry."

"And I depended on you."

"I'm sorry."

"And here you are. You didn't walk away. You didn't let me down. Thank you."

He didn't react to that. He didn't know how to.

"Alex, I'm sorry I didn't have the chance to be a better father to you. I would have liked that. I would have liked to take some credit for the man you've become. It doesn't have to be too late for that, does it?" He followed the fragile question with a slow extension of his hand.

Xander stared down at the outstretched offer of forgiveness and connection, his every muscle paralyzed into immobility. Until the offer was reluctantly withdrawn.

"It's all right, Alex. I understand," Evan Sanders told him softly. "I guess it was too late a long time ago."

Xander lifted his eyes, wide, panicked like something wild run to ground, but not wary. And very slowly, he reached up to put his hands on the sleeves of his stepfather's prison uniform. Fingers clutching tight. He took an awkward step forward, head lowering, cheek resting hesitantly on one of the older man's shoulders. His breath expelled as his father enveloped him in a firm embrace. And his weary eyes slid shut.

"How's Karen?"

Mel settled into the seat of the truck, giving the driver a grateful smile and nod. "Good. She's doing good. Charley says she really likes the new doctor."

"Did they say when she can have visitors?"

"In a couple of weeks."

"Count me in."

"Thanks, Quinn. She'll be glad to see you."

"That's a really nice place you got her into," Quinn was saying, not saying what he really meant. Expensive. Way too expensive for them. Yet the bill had been paid, in advance, quietly and completely through the court. The same way several other of her debts had simply disappeared. Without her knowledge or consent. As if money was no object.

Apparently not where guilt was concerned. And Xander Caufield's must have come with a lot of zeroes attached.

I love you, Mel.

Apparently not enough to do anything about it personally.

She didn't notice their destination until the truck rocked to a stop. Flashes of neon reflected in her shiny eyes as she said softly, "Not tonight, Quinn. I'm not in the mood."

"Then it's the right place to be. C'mon. I'll stand you to a round then I'll take you home if you still want to go."

Where she had nothing, no one waiting. One quick drink. She could withstand the memories for at least that long.

It never ceased to amaze her that after fighting fires all day, her crew would choose to linger in the smoke-filled atmosphere of the bar. They clustered together at the far bend, the less steady spilling over into several tables pushed up close. She had begun to smile at the sound of Teddy Greenbaum's enthusiastic storytelling when her glance caught on an empty chair angled up to the table serving as a footstool for a black high-top-clad foot.

She jerked to a stop, her heart skidding to a similar shuddering halt. Quinn grinned wide.

"Forgot to tell you. You've got company, girl."

Her breath escaped in a rush, but before she could start forward, a firm hand gripped her elbow, propelling her away from where she wanted to go. Her objecting stare lifted to the unexpected sight of Kyle D'Angelo. He didn't express any pleasure in seeing her, either.

"What are you doing here?"

"I'm going to complete this token dance then drink, then drink a lot more then go back to what's left of the Birches and hopefully pass out."

She smiled wryly because his tone was so fierce. "Quite a plan. I meant, why are you still here in Tahoe?"

"A friend of mine talked me into a business venture. He may be a fool when it comes to his affections, but I've never known him to make a bad investment." He stopped at the edge of the dance floor. The song was a slow emotional wailer made for snuggling close. Kyle D'Angelo held her at a cautious arm's length. His steps were awkward, his posture unnaturally stiff.

"Are you all right?"

"Bad back. Aggravated by falling down stairs. I'll be fine as soon as I wash my pain meds down with a little JD on ice."

"A bad combination."

"I can think of worse."

As harsh as his words were to hear, Mel didn't take offense. She knew why he said them. "If we're going to fight, you might as well start on your coma now and spare me the aggravation."

He didn't smile or scowl. His look was unhappily pensive. "I told him it wasn't a good idea. But you know Alex.

Once he gets his mind set on something, there's no derailing him from that straight line toward what he wants."

Her pulse fluttered. "And what does he want?" She tried to maneuver her partner around so she could see the bar and hopefully get a glimpse of the gorgeously aloof man who manipulated her waking hours and stole her dreams. Moving Kyle was like trying to tow a barge with a bicycle.

"He wants to rebuild the Birches."

"Why?" More importantly, did that mean he was staying?

"He's setting his dad up to manage it until he gets his feet back under him. Evan's got a smart head for business. Both him and Alex. They'll be good for each other."

"Oh."

"And he said something about needing a place to hang a pair of watercolors he picked up, or something like that."

A pair...

"And?" she prompted brusquely. "What else does he want?"

His glare narrowed. "Are you going to break his heart?"

"No," she vowed gently, "I'm not."

"Then you'd better ask him yourself."

"Ask me what?"

Kyle spun her under the bridge of his arm, sending her flush against Xander's chest. She froze, unable to summon a single coherent thought except how gorgeous he was. Her memory had failed to capture that breathtaking quality. He waited a patient moment for her to reply then glance at Kyle, who splayed his hands wide and started for the tables.

"Kyle?"

He glanced back at Mel.

"Thanks for keeping your promise." For keeping him safe.

His handsome features softened. "No problem."

Another ballad started up on the jukebox and Xander moved her easily, if at an impersonal distance, to its rhythm. He held her uplifted gaze with one that gave nothing away.

Too nervous to broach any meaningful topic, Mel began with a gruff observation. "You've been paying my bills."

"I have."

"Stop it."

Just a slight flicker behind his eyes then his mild reply. "If that's what you want."

"I don't want to be a charity case."

"Is that how you think I see you? You couldn't be more wrong." When she didn't refute it right away, he stopped and began to pull back. There was no way Mel was going to let him go. She caught his forearms, holding tight, refusing to allow his physical retreat. After a brief stalemate, his arms came up to curve loosely about her again and they resumed their swaying.

"I'm not good at accepting gifts gracefully," she admitted.

"Get used to it."

"I don't like you spending so much on my family. You don't owe us anything."

"It's not about the money, Mel." He sounded upset, even a bit angry. Until she took a step in closer. She heard him inhale, breathing her in slowly, deeply. They still weren't touching except at hand, waist and shoulder. He was wearing a black vee-neck pullover. The silky fabric slid sensuously between her palm and his skin, inviting other smoky thoughts to intrude. His exhalation shook, then his voice was all smooth, calm surface once again. "I want to do for you and yours because I can. Because I want to. Not for any other reason."

"Okay." She settled her head on his shoulder, eyes closing because it felt so natural to be there. Instead of drawing her up against him, his posture grew more tense and self-denying. Everything inside her quivered, but her tone remained carefully neutral. "Kyle told me you were investing in the Birches. It's a nice property, or it will be. Does that mean you'll be stopping in once in a while?"

"No."

She tucked her chin, biting her lips to keep silent. *Don't leave me, Alex. Please don't leave me.*

"I'll be living there, Mel. I'm making it my home. It's time I made my life a little more…peaceful. Alexander the First asked me, no pleaded with me actually, to straighten out the family accounts. I can work here, take on some side projects, keep busy. A lot fewer people tried to beat me up when I was just a simple geek."

She slipped her arms about his waist, nuzzling his neck, sneaking under his defensive radar to whisper, "It's that inner geek I fell in love with. Even though the outer package is pretty damned spectacular, too."

"What did you say? I couldn't hear you over the music."

"I love you, Alex," she murmured, conviction gathering strength with each repetition.

"What?"

"I SAID I LOVE YOU, ALEX."

The music had stopped. Her shouted declaration hung on the smoke-laden air for a long silent minute until Teddy Greenbaum hollered, "About freaking time."

Levering her away, Xander glanced about, choosing to ignore Kyle D'Angelo's mock salute with his glass. His features were closed down tight, his reply to her low and taut.

"Perhaps we should take this someplace a bit more private."

Face flaming, Mel followed him from the dance floor, heading not toward their group of combined friends, but toward the kitchen area. He was moving well, his limp hardly noticeable. She hesitated when he pushed open the door to the small employee restroom but bravely preceded him in. The darkness was complete.

"Did you mean it?" he asked quietly.

"Didn't I say it loudly enough? Was there something else you wanted to hear?"

"Maybe something like I would crawl naked over broken glass for you. I can't sleep nights or form a rational thought because I've missed you so much. I would lay down my life, surrender up my soul, give all that I am and it still wouldn't be enough to be worthy of you."

She chuckled nervously. "Goodness. I must think very highly of you, indeed. I was supposed to say all that?"

"No. I was," he confessed, "a long time ago."

She reached out blindly, her fingertips finding his mouth, pressing there to seal it shut. "Wait," she insisted. "Turn on the light."

They both blinked against the uncompromising brightness. There was no sign of the speaker of those tender sentiments in the properly composed features of Xander Caufield. His lips were compressed into a firm line, his eyes intense, deep, fathomless. His lids drooped slightly as her palm grazed his jaw.

He swallowed hard.

"There's only one thing I want from you right now. The rest we can discuss later."

"What do you want?"

"Four words, Alex. You said them once before. I want to hear them now. I want to look into your eyes when you say them."

His hands found hers, balling them up within their greater size, crushing them unintentionally with their greater strength. He was silent for so long, she wondered if he understood what she was asking of him. And then he said them, the four words that snared her heart.

"I love you, Mel."

She closed her eyes, taking an instant to savor the sound.

"Can I tell you that every day for the rest of my life?" Xander asked.

"You'd better."

His expression relaxed into a genuine smile that warmed his eyes and did wonderful, rhythm-altering things to her pulse rate. "I'm uptight, compulsive, I'm arrogant and I'll want my own way even when it's not the right way and I don't deserve it. Don't take any crap off me."

"I don't cook. I clean only if I can't step over or around it. I snore and I like to hog all the hot water," she responded.

"We can shower together. I recall enjoying that very much."

Her heart shuddered. "Alex, are you sure about this? Look at me." She glanced down at her worn khakis, work boots and baggy camp shirt. "I'm not going to fit into your world."

"I'm looking. I like what I see. And I like the fit."

"Kyle doesn't like me."

"I don't shower with Kyle." He bumped up against her, nudging her back against the cool edge of the sink. "Can I go home with you?" His voice was a husky rip of emotion.

"I insist on it." She leaned forward so their lips could meet and mesh for a fleeting moment.

In a deeper rumble, he asked, "Can I boff you right here on the sink first?"

"I'm afraid I'm going to have to insist on that, too."

He kissed her. The slow, sweet seduction of her senses weakened her will and left her knees wobbly. He boosted her up onto the tiled basin rim without lessening that soul-stirring pressure. Then she felt his smile against her mouth.

"I'm Alex. Fly me."

Her arms went about his neck.

And they both flew.

Dante Raintree stood with his arms crossed as he watched the woman on the monitor. The image was in black and white to better show details; color distracted the brain. He focused on her hands, watching every move she made, but what struck him most was how uncommonly *still* she was. She didn't fidget or play with her chips, or look around at the other players. She peeked once at her down card, then didn't touch it again, signaling for another hit by tapping a fingernail on the table. Just because she didn't seem to be paying attention to the other players, though, didn't mean she was as unaware as she seemed.

"What's her name?" Dante asked.

"Lorna Clay," replied his chief of security, Al Rayburn.

"At first I thought she was counting, but she doesn't pay enough attention."

"She's paying attention, all right," Dante murmured. "You just don't see her doing it." A card counter had to remember every card played. Supposedly counting cards was impossible with the number of decks used by the casinos, but there were those rare individuals who could calculate the odds even with multiple decks.

"I thought that, too," said Al. "But look at this piece of tape coming up. Someone she knows comes up to her and speaks, she looks around and starts chatting, completely misses the play of the people to her left—and doesn't look around even when the deal comes back to her, just taps that finger. And damn if she didn't win. Again."

Dante watched the tape, rewound it, watched it again. Then he watched it a third time. There had to be something he was missing, because he couldn't pick out a single giveaway.

"If she's cheating," Al said with something like respect, "she's the best I've ever seen."

"What does your gut say?"

Al scratched the side of his jaw, considering. Finally, he said, "If she isn't cheating, she's the luckiest person walking. She wins. Week in, week out, she wins. Never a huge amount, but I ran the numbers and she's into us for about five grand a week. Hell, boss, on her way out of the casino she'll stop by a slot machine, feed a dollar in and walk away with at least fifty. It's never the same machine, either. I've had her watched, I've had her followed, I've even looked for the same faces in the casino every time she's in here, and I can't find a common denominator."

"Is she here now?"

"She came in about half an hour ago. She's playing black-jack, as usual."

"Bring her to my office," Dante said, making a swift decision. "Don't make a scene."

"Got it," said Al, turning on his heel and leaving the security center.

Dante left, too, going up to his office. His face was calm. Normally he would leave it to Al to deal with a cheater, but he was curious. How was she doing it? There were a lot of bad cheaters, a few good ones, and every so often one would come along who was the stuff of which legends were made: the cheater who didn't get caught, even when people were alert and the camera was on him—or, in this case, her.

It was possible to simply be lucky, as most people understood luck. Chance could turn a habitual loser into a big-time winner. Casinos, in fact, thrived on that hope. But luck itself wasn't habitual, and he knew that what passed for luck was often something else: cheating. And there was the other kind of luck, the kind he himself possessed, but it depended not on chance but on who and what he was. He knew it was an innate power and not Dame Fortune's erratic smile. Since power like his was rare, the odds made it likely the woman he'd been watching was merely a very clever cheat.

Her skill could provide her with a very good living, he thought, doing some swift calculations in his head. Five grand a week equaled $260,000 a year, and that was just from his casino. She probably hit them all, careful to keep the numbers relatively low so she stayed under the radar.

He wondered how long she'd been taking him, how

long she'd been winning a little here, a little there, before Al noticed.

The curtains were open on the wall-to-wall window in his office, giving the impression, when one first opened the door, of stepping out onto a covered balcony. The glazed window faced west, so he could catch the sunsets. The sun was low now, the sky painted in purple and gold. At his home in the mountains, most of the windows faced east, affording him views of the sunrise. Something in him needed both the greeting and the goodbye of the sun. He'd always been drawn to sunlight, maybe because fire was his element to call, to control.

He checked his internal time: four minutes until sundown. Without checking the sunrise tables every day, he knew exactly when the sun would slide behind the mountains. He didn't own an alarm clock. He didn't need one. He was so acutely attuned to the sun's position that he had only to check within himself to know the time. As for waking at a particular time, he was one of those people who could tell himself to wake at a certain time, and he did. That talent had nothing to do with being Raintree, so he didn't have to hide it; a lot of perfectly ordinary people had the same ability.

He had other talents and abilities, however, that did require careful shielding. The long days of summer instilled in him an almost sexual high, when he could feel contained power buzzing just beneath his skin. He had to be doubly careful not to cause candles to leap into flame just by his presence, or to start wildfires with a glance in the dry-as-tinder brush. He loved Reno; he didn't want to burn it down. He just felt so damn *alive* with all the sunshine pouring down that he wanted to let the energy pour through him instead of holding it inside.

This must be how his brother Gideon felt while pulling lightning, all that hot power searing through his muscles, his veins. They had this in common, the connection with raw power. All the members of the far-flung Raintree clan had some power, some heightened ability, but only members of the royal family could channel and control the earth's natural energies.

Dante wasn't just of the royal family, he was the Dranir, the leader of the entire clan. "Dranir" was synonymous with king, but the position he held wasn't ceremonial, it was one of sheer power. He was the oldest son of the previous Dranir, but he would have been passed over for the position if he hadn't also inherited the power to hold it.

Behind him came Al's distinctive knock on the door. The outer office was empty, Dante's secretary having gone home hours before. "Come in," he called, not turning from his view of the sunset.

The door opened, and Al said, "Mr. Raintree, this is Lorna Clay."

Dante turned and looked at the woman, all his senses on alert. The first thing he noticed was the vibrant color of her hair, a rich, dark red that encompassed a multitude of shades from copper to burgundy. The warm amber light danced along the iridescent strands, and he felt a hard tug of sheer lust in his gut. Looking at her hair was almost like looking at fire, and he had the same reaction.

The second thing he noticed was that she was spitting mad.

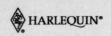

Silhouette®
ROMANTIC SUSPENSE

**Sparked by Danger,
Fueled by Passion.**

This month and every month look for
four new heart-racing romances
set against a backdrop of suspense!

Available in May 2007

Safety in Numbers
(Wild West Bodyguards miniseries)
by Carla Cassidy

Jackson's Woman
by Maggie Price

Shadow Warrior
(Night Guardians miniseries)
by Linda Conrad

One Cool Lawman
by Diane Pershing

Available wherever you buy books!

Visit Silhouette Books at www.eHarlequin.com

SRS0407

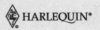

Mediterranean
NIGHTS™

Tycoon Elias Stamos is launching his newest luxury cruise ship from his home port in Greece. But someone from his past is eager to expose old secrets and to see the Stamos empire crumble.

Mediterranean Nights
launches in June 2007 with...

FROM RUSSIA, WITH LOVE
by *Ingrid Weaver*

Join the guests and crew of *Alexandra's Dream* as they are drawn into a world of glamour, romance and intrigue in this new 12-book series.

REQUEST YOUR FREE BOOKS!

2 FREE NOVELS PLUS 2 FREE GIFTS!

Silhouette® Romantic

SUSPENSE

Sparked by Danger, Fueled by Passion!

YES! Please send me 2 FREE Silhouette® Romantic Suspense novels and my 2 FREE gifts. After receiving them, if I don't wish to receive any more books, I can return the shipping statement marked "cancel." If I don't cancel, I will receive 4 brand-new novels every month and be billed just $4.24 per book in the U.S., or $4.99 per book in Canada, plus 25¢ shipping and handling per book plus applicable taxes, if any*. That's a savings of at least 15% off the cover price! I understand that accepting the 2 free books and gifts places me under no obligation to buy anything. I can always return a shipment and cancel at any time. Even if I never buy another book from Silhouette, the two free books and gifts are mine to keep forever.

240 SDN EEX6 340 SDN EEYJ

Name	(PLEASE PRINT)	
Address		Apt. #
City	State/Prov.	Zip/Postal Code

Signature (if under 18, a parent or guardian must sign)

Mail to the Silhouette Reader Service™:
IN U.S.A.: P.O. Box 1867, Buffalo, NY 14240-1867
IN CANADA: P.O. Box 609, Fort Erie, Ontario L2A 5X3

Not valid to current Silhouette Intimate Moments subscribers.

Want to try two free books from another line?
Call 1-800-873-8635 or visit www.morefreebooks.com.

* Terms and prices subject to change without notice. NY residents add applicable sales tax. Canadian residents will be charged applicable provincial taxes and GST. This offer is limited to one order per household. All orders subject to approval. Credit or debit balances in a customer's account(s) may be offset by any other outstanding balance owed by or to the customer. Please allow 4 to 6 weeks for delivery.

Your Privacy: Silhouette is committed to protecting your privacy. Our Privacy Policy is available online at www.eHarlequin.com or upon request from the Reader Service. From time to time we make our lists of customers available to reputable firms who may have a product or service of interest to you. If you would prefer we not share your name and address, please check here. ☐

SRS07

Silhouette®

Romantic

SUSPENSE

COMING NEXT MONTH

#1463 SAFETY IN NUMBERS—Carla Cassidy
Wild West Bodyguards
Chase McCall arrives in Cotter Creek to investigate the powerful entity of bodyguards known as the West family and immediately strikes an attraction for the lone female of the bunch. Can Chase keep his cool while exploring these possible murder suspects?

#1464 JACKSON'S WOMAN—Maggie Price
Dates with Destiny
U.S. special agent Jackson Castle watched Claire Munroe walk away from him once. Now his ex-partner vows vengeance on him by going after the only woman he's ever loved…and Jackson is all that stands between Claire and a cold-blooded killer.

#1465 SHADOW WARRIOR—Linda Conrad
Night Guardians
Tradition demands that Michael Ayze marry his brother's widow—the woman he's forbidden to love. Will Michael resist temptation and still protect Alexis from the evil shapeshifters who will use her for ill?

#1466 ONE COOL LAWMAN—Diane Pershing
Can an L.A. detective fight his attraction to the mother of a kidnapped girl long enough to uncover the perpetrator? In doing so, he's risking his life—but can he also handle risking his heart?